Like a Summer
Never to Be Repeated

Like a Summer
Never to Be Repeated

Mohamed Berrada

Translated by
Christina Phillips

The American University in Cairo Press
Cairo   New York

This paperback edition published in 2015 by
The American University in Cairo Press
113 Sharia Kasr el Aini, Cairo, Egypt
420 Fifth Avenue, New York, NY 10018
www.aucpress.com

Exclusive distribution outside Egypt and North America by I.B. Tauris & Co Ltd.,
6 Salem Road, London, W4 2BU

Dar el Kutub No. 7553/15
ISBN 978 977 416 735 5

Dar el Kutub Cataloging-in-Publication Data

Berrada, Mohamed
        Like a Summer Never to Be Repeated / Mohamed Berrada.—Cairo:
    The American University in Cairo Press, 2015.
            p.   cm.
        ISBN 978 977 416 735 5
        1. English fiction
        823

1 2 3 4 5   19 18 17 16 15

Designed by Adam el Sehemy
Printed in Egypt

To my friends in Egypt: too many for me to count.
And to Leila, I dedicate to you these tales of Egypt,
whose love also brought us together.

Part One
Holes Unceasingly Filled

Memories are a betrayal of nature
Because the nature of yesterday isn't Nature.
What was is nothing, and to remember is to not see.
Pass by, bird: pass by and teach me.

—Fernando Pessoa

The Threshold of
Bab al-Hadid Station

HAMMAD READ WHAT HE had written on a white sheet of paper ten years earlier:

> Bab al-Hadid Square. August. The midday sun blazed as he stepped out of the train station in Cairo, his suitcase in one hand and a cardboard box containing a dark blue suit he bought the night he left Paris for Rome in the other. He wasn't yet seventeen. . . .

He paused for a moment and let his thoughts wander: Why begin with Bab al-Hadid Square? Wouldn't it have been better to begin with his family's farewell in Rabat or with boarding the boat in Casablanca on July 13, 1955 heading for Marseille, or at dawn in the train station in Paris on his way to Rome?

There were many possible beginnings. Hammad supposed that the clamoring image of Bab al-Hadid Square, swelling with activity, cars, the yellow tram, and people, had lodged itself in his mind, especially after he had arrived there several times and seen it in the film *Bab al-Hadid* depicted from a perspective that blended reality with the dreams and illusions of the sensual actress Hind Rostom, with her relaxed, light-footed gait. Besides, there was no absolute beginning, he said to himself. What he was going to write was clothed with imagination, interjected in time and space, and constructed from words. And it would soon be razed by other memories as they burst out suddenly from some corner of his unconscious. He thought a little and added: I'll write what I remember then edit it and embellish it creatively until I have an ample account, into which I'll have woven all that insists on inhabiting the page lest it fade in my memory.

Hammad was almost seventeen when he decided to travel to Cairo to finish school, as Arabic education in the private schools set up by the Nationalist Movement did not include the baccalaureate and tightened French authority meant it was limited.

If he chose Cairo rather than Damascus, as others had, it was because of the many scenes his memory had accumulated from films like *Long Live Love*, *Forbidden Love*, and *Love and Revenge* and songs by Abd al-Wahhab, Farid al-Atrash, Asmahan, and Umm Kulthum. The names of certain writers—Taha Hussein, Tawfiq al-Hakim, al-Manfaluti, and Ahmad Lutfi al-Sayyid—had also snuck into his soul through the reading he undertook on his own in Bab Shala Library, close to Muhammad V School. Only now, as he walked out into Bab al-Hadid Square carrying his suitcase and suit in the scorching August sun and clamor of the street, the like of which he had never experienced in quiet Rabat, did he understand that he was entering an unknown world which bore no relation to the city he saw in those chic, romantic films. He looked right and left and turned around, following the brown figures in gallabiyas of all colors with cotton skullcaps on their heads despite the heat, the women, who were mostly wearing black milayas, and a few men in European-style suits and red tarbooshes. It was a very different mix to the one he had left behind in his own country. There was also the yellow tram that cut through the middle of the square, and the pushcarts and bicycles that never seemed to stop. He tried to ask for the address of the North African Lodge where a friend who had arrived a year earlier was staying. He used what classical Arabic he knew to ask a man in a striped gallabiya with a white turban on his head, "How do I get to the North African Lodge in Agouza, please?" He spoke quickly and falteringly and the man had to ask him to clarify what he was saying a number of times. The exchange failed so he tried again with other people. Passersby gathered round to get a good look at this guy who appeared to be an Arab but couldn't speak Arabic. When Hammad recalled that awful episode, he couldn't remember exactly how he finally got to the North African Lodge in Agouza or how he handled being lost before finding his friend Nabih, who embraced him warmly and cried, "Cairo celebrates. Welcome. Praise God you're well." The words coming out of Nabih's mouth had the same accent as the people Hammad had spoken to in Bab al-Hadid Square and heard in films. So his friend, who was laughing loudly and slapping his back exuberantly, had mastered the Egyptian dialect. Nabih laughed a lot as he listened to Hammad's account of Bab al-Hadid Square and his problems communicating. "Don't worry," he said, "We'll teach you Egyptian in a week. You'll be a nightingale. No offense but, as they say in Morocco, you're like an Arab in a strange land!" Some students began to emerge from their rooms to say hello and ask about affairs in Morocco and news of the struggle. One of them was Abd al-Qadir. He was tall, slim, and good-looking with smooth brown skin. Hammad quickly recognized him, for he had been the hero of a romance at the Muhammad V School before traveling to Egypt. He had acquired a reputation after writing a letter to a pupil he liked, which began, "Love dropped from the sky. You must acknowledge it." The pupils passed the letter around secretly and watched the two of them walking among the other girls and boys in the fifth form. There would be further romances for Abd al-Qadir in Cairo, for he seemed made to dress elegantly, flirt with girls, and stay up late as was the custom in Cairo.

When Hammad asked his friend Nabih about a student called Barhum, whether he had arrived yet from Morocco, Nabih said he had turned up a month ago with his friend Alaa. Their risky attempt to escape on foot to "North Morocco" had been a success. Hammad was delighted. He had made friends with Barhum through an exchange of letters after reading a prose poem of his in a Moroccan magazine and finding it echoed some of his personal feelings. They met up in Rabat and formed a strong friendship through mutual literary interests and the prospect of escaping to Egypt: Hammad via a trip to France organized by the Department for Youth and Sport, which was under French supervision, and his friend across the borders between the two Moroccos of the time: Spain and France.

In the evening, Barhum returned from the cinema to a surprise, and years full of talk and banter began. When he introduced him to his friend Alaa, the trio that would live and do everything together for the next five years—and survive beyond through friendship and shared memories—was complete.

These moments and scenes of novelty and humor floated on the surface of Hammad's memory. But when he tried to picture them it was as though they had been filtered through a sieve. For instance, he couldn't recall the complicated process of getting into the Husayniya School to prepare for the tawjihiya but had a good, clear recollection of meeting Barhum in a café on Ataba Square in the first week of September in order to go together to a friend who had already passed it to get some of his books.

Hammad arrived a little before six in the evening and sat at a table at the far end of the long passage that ran parallel to Azbakiya Garden. Barhum arrived a few moments later, with the waiter coming to take their order behind him. "Two teas please," one of them said. They looked at each other as if to say that sitting here like this was rather extravagant for people who count their piasters and milliemes and expect the family cheque from Morocco to be delayed. They quickly agreed to leave without waiting for the tea weighing heavily on their budget. As they got up and made their way toward Azbakiya Garden, the waiter appeared through the café door at the other end of the passage. They broke into a run. They could hear the voice of the waiter hurrying after them, "Your tea, sirs," and then shouting (when he was sure they were trying to escape), "Your tea, you sons of bitches!" at the top of his voice.

The North African Lodge brought together students from Algeria, Tunisia, and 'Marrakech,' and received aid from the Arab University so it could house students wanting to continue studying in Arabic. The living conditions were not great but it provided shelter, the opportunity to meet people, and support. Like a gift from heaven, the Moroccan actor al-Doghmi had also emigrated to Cairo and enrolled at the Institute of Drama. Hammad knew him from watching some of his early plays at gatherings, wedding celebrations, and the theater in Morocco. Plays like *Truth Manifested and Falsehood Perished* and *The Orphan*, which were aimed at raising consciousness and spreading the message of the nationalist movement and which unveiled a young talent who channeled all his energy into the national struggle. The man was a model of self-sacrifice in the service of others and a firm believer that Arabic education was fundamental to the continuing struggle and to confronting the burdens of independence. Thus he took it upon himself to help every newly arrived student. He would guide him through the labyrinths of the government building on Tahrir Square, register him at the North African Arab Bureau on Abd al-Khaliq Tharwat Street, and lend him money while he waited for provisions from his family. He took particular care of students from Rabat, probably because he knew their families and shared the same background. He was quick to establish a weekly tradition of gathering the students from Rabat every Friday at lunchtime in the small apartment he shared with a friend to enjoy a rich meal, which would include kebabs and kofta, and exchange news about Morocco and the fight for independence. Hammad was not, strictly speaking, from Rabat but his friendships and the fact that he had lived there permitted him to attend the Friday banquet. He tried to urge his Kenitra friends to establish a similar ritual but they did not have a father figure like al-Doghmi. There were no city boundaries in the house of the leader Allal al-Fassi in Heliopolis, however, where the students would meet to have tea and sweet pastries and apprise news of the country from its sources. There began to be a sense that negotiations with France for the return of the exiled king and an independence agreement were imminent, but there were a number of fears. The leader was not convinced about independence with continued 'ties' and the Liberation Army was keen to expand and eliminate the French presence in the south. It was a hopeful beginning but filled with anxiety and apprehension. Still, the most important thing for Hammad and his friends right now was to get through the tawjihiya and start university.

The Husayniya School in Abbasiya was famous for its headmaster, whom the pupils nicknamed "The Beast" after the hero of a well-known radio series. He was tall with sunken eyes, a fiery glare, and gray hair. Old age lined his temples and his voice was loud and firm, and he always walked with his hands held behind his back. He was never satisfied with scolding and dishing out punishments, and was known to grab a pupil by the

8

scruff of his neck, lift him like a feather, and fling him toward the door. Hammad and his Moroccan friends at the Husayniya School had a history of mischief but their special situation and the hopes pinned on them, as well as the tyranny of "The Beast," ensured they behaved themselves and obeyed orders by the administration and teachers. Nevertheless, there was opposition to authority in the classroom, where the Egyptian pupils had an incredible supply of jokes and ways of harassing the teacher; their antagonism was quite remorseless. The classes of the Arabic language teacher Abd al-Samie Effendi were a time for impromptu scenes that invigorated the soul and set tongues loose. Ustaz Abd al-Samie was really a nice guy. He was quite fat and his stomach stuck out bashfully. He wore spectacles and a red tarboosh, and swayed a little as he walked. He was traditional and his method of teaching was not very effective, for he would spend the class dictating the rules of grammar and correcting mistakes. The North African pupils would memorize the rules and observe them in writing and speech whereas the Egyptians paid little attention, except for one boy who was preparing to be a public speaker and who in oratory class would improvise sonorous discourses unspoiled by the barbarism in front of and behind him.

Two weeks after school started Ustaz Abd al-Samie asked the North African pupils to bring in photographs of themselves so they could get school identification cards. He kept asking and they kept ignoring him, so he summoned a pupil, the tallest in the class, who was also rather large, and said, "Abd al-Rahman, take your brothers' pictures and give them to me tomorrow." From that day on they agreed on Abd al-Rahman as their leader, whose job it would be to represent them before the administration and protect their interests. The choice was also motivated by the fact that Abd al-Rahman, who came from Fakik in eastern Morocco, was fond of memorizing Gamal Abd al-Nasser's speeches and imitating his delivery. They would gather round him in the schoolyard and common room at the North African Lodge and demand extracts from the leader's speeches. Gradually the fooling about in Arabic class spread beyond the Egyptians and the two groups began to interact: all the hostility disappeared and the North Africans started to join in. Abd al-Samie liked to end each class repeating his mantra for the pupils: "If each of you memorizes the texts and rules well you'll understand them properly. You'll speak without grammatical mistakes and be polite and respectful of principles. You'll be first-class. You'll be what? You'll be what?"

Tongues would race to answer. "A hero. A respected hero. The top student in Egypt. The son of his mother and father."

One day Ustaz Abd al-Samie directed the question to Hammad, "What will you be, Hammad?"

"Unique!"

"Great! Bravo! You've begun to talk like your Egyptian brothers."

There was also Abd al-Muhsin, the history teacher, who came as something of a shock to Hammad. He was large and had a round face, wide jaw, fair hair, and a loud, talkative voice. He stood out because he delivered his lessons in colloquial Egyptian, waving his hands about nonstop as he circled the pupils' desks. Ustaz Abd al-Muhsin would not put up with passive listening and nodding heads. He would stir up the pupils and surprise them with questions about what he had said. He had a gift for storytelling and succeeded in bringing to life the various phases and critical moments of the French Revolution. Whenever Hammad remembered him his remarks on the Battle of Waterloo would come to mind: "Napoleon came and told them that this won't do. I won't let you build your nest behind my back. What did he say? He said, 'This isn't acceptable. I'm an emperor not just a king and I do what I want. You want to surround me and take my empire to pieces but you never will.'"

"What did he say to them?" Abd al-Muhsin sprang the question on Hammad.

"He said, sir, that this isn't acceptable. I'm an emperor. . . ."

"Who did he say it to?"

"You didn't say who he said it to, sir."

"You're supposed to know. I told you last week to read about the Battle of Waterloo in your history book. Sit, Moroccan boy, sit down."

Ustaz Abd al-Muhsin continued, "On June 18, 1915 the Battle of Waterloo took place between Napoleon and the British and Prussian forces. It was the battle in which he met his doom and which forced him to abdicate and go into exile on the island of St. Helena." He wrote the date of the battle on the blackboard and put a circle round it then banged his fat fist down three times, "This was the end of your Uncle Napoleon who humbled Europe for more than fifteen years!"

Did It
Really Happen?

HAMMAD REREAD WHAT HE had written and became immersed in thought. He had ignored several details, or they had escaped him at the time of writing. He hadn't written enough about Nabih, for they were friends before traveling to Cairo and he had kept up with him after the tawjihiya and declaration of Moroccan independence, when Nabih decided to go to France and study commerce. Nabih was older than Hammad and often made controversial decisions, such as in the last year of primary school when he arrived one morning with his head completely shaved—totally bald—because his brother-in-law had convinced him that 'la frizzé' was unlawful in Islam and deviated from the customs of the umma. In Cairo, Hammad found Nabih Egyptianized, no longer speaking in the North African dialect and denying that he had any affiliation other than to Egypt and its people. Four years later, when he met Nabih in Morocco after he had obtained his diploma from the Higher Institute of Commerce in Paris, he found a different person again. He had adopted a French manner of speaking and dressing and did not want to discuss his time in Cairo. All his conversation revolved around profitability and the allocation of time, effort, friendship, and conversation; even the extent to which the clothes he bought would last had to be calculated. Moreover, when he related the story of his marriage to the French girl Henriette, he said that he was not concerned with beauty or elegance (indeed, Henriette resembled a white, fleshy, fat pig) but her ability to live without expensive health problems and to yield high profits! After that meeting the two men grew apart, perhaps because Hammad found Nabih's transformation absurd and shocking, though he later reproached himself for neglecting his friend's news, especially when he heard about him at the ministry of commerce and how he had refused to enter into the game of bribery and government employee remuneration. When he visited him in hospital after a difficult operation, Nabih was someone else again, yearning to restore relations with his family, whom he had lost touch with because of his French wife, longing for his friends from childhood and youth, and afraid of separation and death. I made a mistake, Hammad said to himself. Even if he didn't deserve friendship, he deserved the novelist's curiosity. Nabih was fickle; he would look and speak one way then switch to another. Isn't that natural? What was wrong then? Who has the right to judge? Can we follow the lives of everyone we have ever known? Where would we find the time and energy? Yet we often find ourselves alone and unconsciously begin inventing phases and destinies for people whom we knew and then vanished from sight. Is it true that when we met in the North African Lodge in Cairo Nabih laughed loudly and said, "As we say, you're like an Arab in a strange land?" Hammad suddenly asked himself. Did he really take him with him on a rendezvous one evening to Qasr al-Nil Casino and introduce him to a girl called Fawziya,

13

who had brown skin, honey-colored eyes, and delicate features and spoke in a whisper? Did Nabih really say to her at the end of the meeting, "I want you to keep an eye on Ustaz Hammad. He is still fresh. We want him to loosen up a bit"? And did Fawziya really point to her eyes with her fingers and give Hammad a collusive look?

Did it really happen that, coming back from the Husayniya School one afternoon, a group of Moroccan friends left him asleep on the tram, alighting at Agouza while he stayed on until the conductor woke him at the last stop in Imbaba, and that he had started swearing and cursing and thinking up ways to exact revenge? Repayment was swift, for he patiently endured the ridicule and mockery after arriving back at the North African Lodge by foot and put on a show of anger until he discovered that Abduh, who was proud and laughing loudly, had been the ringleader. The next morning Hammad sneaked up to the box in which Abduh hid the apple and orange that he usually ate before breakfast, on the instructions of his mother, who sent him a special budget for morning fruit, and stole them before he woke up and discovered them missing. Hammad maintained his angry façade and wouldn't answer Abduh's questions. Barhum couldn't help laughing as they assured him that a ghost had got the apple and orange while they were asleep. His memories were like foam that rises to the surface of the Nile or a match that you watch in a light whirlpool until it disappears. . . . Like what else? Like chrysolite glistening. Like a sudden breeze amid the midday heat. Like innumerable things that appear all at once and come between us and the things we want to understand and possess the clearest possible picture of.

Hammad hovered around everything that appeared to him, distant or close up, through the holes in the sieve of time, or rather through the holes in the layers of time upon which dust or a kind of rust had settled. His soul throbbed with temptation and fascination. His journey was a bridge, a crossing to another place. But he was not aware, as he entered it, of the thunderbolt that invaded his being and memory. He could no longer remember what happened to that innocence that responded to his lively inner outburst, an outburst that didn't yield to any system or logic—powerful and irresistible. He clung to a destiny which it became impossible to let go of once he had set foot in Cairo and heard the sound, the noise, and the melodic, elongated, relaxed words and conversations of the midday lull. For many years he thought of Cairo as continuous clamor, as noise and stray sounds, synchronizing in the air to lend this eternally speaking space its essential character.

On a recent visit Hammad had an unexpected and confusing experience. He was in a car with a friend, who was driving slowly, on the way back from a trip to al-Qarafa, a city where the dead and the living live together in harmony. The sun was setting as the car descended through the belt of Manshiyat Nasser and both of them were silent. Hammad suddenly felt as though the noise had disappeared, as though the sounds had vanished and a sudden calm was encompassing everything around him, or at least the city's lowlands and quarters. For a time the earth and sky and mankind seemed wound in a mantilla of sunset darkness. Small tufts of pink emerged through the creeping darkness, emitting a streaming light that countered the inundating blackness. A fleeting moment of calm, pierced a few moments later by the mellow sound of the muezzin. Everything was still. Was blackness giving chase to the light? Was death declaring its presence? Was it just the never-ending motion?

He contemplated the sensation that had taken hold of him years before and made him understand that we are always pursuing something without knowing what it is. We pursue time, he said to himself, which doesn't pursue us but is happy to watch as we hop about and seldom come to rest on anything. Who was it that said, "The way we hurry the clock and watch its hands—it's death. We're all dead people rushing"?

"His journey was a crossing to another place." Is it possible to count the thresholds that we have crossed on our life journeys? Sometimes we cross a threshold on which we had pinned hope and find a mirage, or it becomes a forgotten memory. Hammad constantly hovered around the threshold of the journey to Cairo without finding clear answers. Where did his intention begin and end? What were the 'crossing points' to this new place? Emotion? Language? The space clamoring with raw narrative?

Emotion? A song that bursts forth suddenly from the unconscious and announces a connection with an everlasting childhood? A fleeting memory that shakes your being, your nerve tissue, and longing for what's passed? Words that furtively etch into your hidden dictionary grooves of intimacy and vaults that lead to the vastness of the universe? A sudden moment that makes you realize that you are not as you imagined, but plural in your oneness and unity. . . . Emotion seemed to be all this, but it was also a slender plant that you colored and draped in a veil, annexing it to the realm of conjecture and the invisible.

From time to time Hammad would wander through the back streets, through the long streets fragrant with the scent of history, bodies, smells, clothes, colors, and marvelous events. Sensations and scenes that reminded him of things he picked up as he rushed through the alleys and markets of old Fez. A game of shadows and colors, a mosaic of lights spreading over the roofs of the markets, skylights, and open shop doors. He walked, eyes open and listening to sounds and fragments of conversation. Behind the Azhar Mosque he went down a sidestreet, toward the fountain where girls and women were filling dark earthenware pitchers. He turned around and caught sight of a large woman sitting in a muddy spot on the ground, the small pits around her filled with leftover rainwater. She was wearing a black gallabiya and her round face was uncovered. She was talking loudly to men sitting by a shop behind her while her hands were busy preparing tea on a gas stove in front of her. He crept closer, amazed by this woman sitting naturally and relaxed in the mud, as though on a sofa stuffed with ostrich feathers, talking, laughing, and responding to the men's remarks. He recalled some snippets: "I warn you. . . . You'll get your just deserts. . . . So? I saw him with my own eyes with a basket of vegetables. . . . You think. . . ."

Hammad watched the whole scene from his hiding place: the woman in the middle of the lane, the empty-looking shops with few commodities, the people sitting on chairs or leaning against the wall, the mud, the groups of donkeys loaded with merchandise passing every now and then, the young women with their seductive glances wrapped in milayas, and the intimacy that soldered the woman with her surroundings so that she did not feel at all shy and onlookers were not even aware she was sitting in the mud. His amazement stayed with him and whenever he remembered the woman he was at a loss to explain his attraction to this intimacy. Years later, listening to a popular song by Abd al-Latif Effendi al-Banna, he smiled as he remembered the woman and pictured her singing the popular tune:

What do you think of my charm?
What do you think of my good humor?
Aren't I delicate?
Aren't I sweet?
Like a nice set of teeth
Like money cannot buy. . . .

She was indeed sweet and charming, and her face, words, and movements emitted that mysterious quality that immediately grabs people.

When Hammad recalled those days, which "floated like foam on the surface of the Nile," he could not follow his memory's logic as it leapt back and forth and he ended up submitting to its whims. He sometimes thought that the holes might be filled if others, everyone he remembered now, had written about that phase, about their so-called "shared memories," so that he could reorganize his memory. But what was the point? Events in themselves did not interest him or other people. Rather he responded to a desire to write, to seize raw materials and knead and transform them, abrogating almost all else but nevertheless retaining echoes of a past whose warm pulse had not completely disappeared. He often paused when he recalled the details of a letter he wrote to a beautiful and intelligent pupil in Rabat after the announcement of Moroccan independence. Perhaps it was her who sent him a description of the excited celebrations and explosion of joy. He remembered well the sober passage he wrote in a sedate tone, draped in gravity, informing her that he was not among those who greeted the momentous event with joy alone; rather, "I sat alone and reflected on what it would mean in the future, when the rejoicing is over and it is time to return to the real world and ask ourselves: Are we ready to bear this enormous responsibility?"

He said to himself that what he had written to the girl was arrogant and conceited, even if it did foretell the crisis post-independence. What use was his prediction? Events and developments follow a more complex logic. And there is also the unexpected, which neither rational analysis nor the laws of history can illuminate. Perhaps he wrote the letter to demonstrate that he was different from others and to dazzle her with the judiciousness he had acquired abroad.

Hammad didn't know why he often remembered the face of the Italian he met on the deck of the steamer from Naples to Alexandria. The Italian talked to him in French and told him that he had been living in Egypt for a while and advised him to steer clear of politics as the new regime did not permit affiliation to any other party. It was a waste of time and it was in Hammad's best interest to focus on his studies so he could be of benefit to his country. His tone was paternal and sympathetic. Hammad made do with nodding his head in agreement. It was difficult to explain the burning emotions that grew inside him as he listened in Rabat to news of the July Revolution, and the enthusiasm that exploded in the hearts of him and his friends who, though young, were involved in political groups attached to the Nationalist Movement. But he saw evidence of what the Italian was talking about in Cairo in the groups that lived perpetually on guard, lying in wait, hiding, and unable to openly voice their hostility to Nasser. The Italian was the first foreigner Hammad met on the deck of the steamer before setting foot in Egypt.

Like what else? Like sad eyes glistening sorrowfully through the smile on a brown face. This was the image his memory took away from his first meeting with Fawziya. Before Nabih left for France he had given Hammad her telephone number and urged him to contact her and inform her of his departure. When he called her voice sounded different and lacked the piercing whisper from before. She familiarized herself with him and asked him to come to her house as her father and husband were away traveling and she was alone and unable to go out. He hesitated for a moment then agreed. She opened the small aperture in the plaited door and when she saw him she smiled happily and quickly opened the door. It was the first time he entered a house in Cairo. The hallway of the flat was filled with furniture, pictures of people, including Nefertiti and the comic actor Naguib al-Rihani, and sofas draped with dark blue covers to protect them from dust. She welcomed him and he smiled in awe and asked if it wasn't too much trouble. Never. Please sit down. She pushed the cover of one of the sofas to the side. "Would you like to drink coffee or tea or something cold?" "No, I've just had something." He was longing to listen to her, to touch her, maybe even undress her. He was fearful and happy to be on his first adventure in the land of the films that had filled his imagination when he went to the cinema in Bab Boujeloud in Fez. He asked her why she was sad and why she was alone in the house and she told him about the schemes of her father's wife, about being orphaned, and giving up school. She asked him about Nabih and he told her that he had left for France and sent his best wishes. "Without even phoning to say goodbye?" "You know Nabih better than me. He's moody. You never said how you met. . . ." "We would see each other at the bus station and smile. One day he spoke to me and asked if we could meet. When I discovered he was Moroccan I wanted to get to know him more. We would meet in Shagara Casino. He would sing me songs by Farid al-Atrash. His voice was very sweet." Hammad recalled the times he had listened to Nabih singing extracts from Farid's songs and imitating his lamentations and tears back in Rabat. She was silent for a little then said, "Never mind, Sayyidi. We wish him luck in France. How are you doing?"

He chatted with her happily in his faltering Egyptian and she corrected some of his pronunciation and encouraged him with her laughter. They held hands and he seemed in a rush, for his previous experiences had all been of a direct nature, focused on lust and devoid of kisses and flirting. Fawziya was different. She guided him slowly and soothed his fervor through touching, stroking, whispering, and a little singing. Her experience, manner of expression, and knowledge of the body's secret places and sensitive spots suggested that she was older than him. But she didn't forget to whisper in his ear, "I'm sure Nabih told you that I'm a virgin and don't want any difficulties." When she took off her blouse and bra Hammad was astounded by the harmony between her honey-colored eyes and brown face, which was framed by black hair, and her chest with its two bedazzling, mellow pears. More enjoyment, or rather enjoyment of a new kind. They arranged to meet again, outside the house. The meetings continued until Hammad started university and yielded to the throng of dates with young girls and women of fleeting pleasure and ambiguous relationships.

Like a Summer
Never to Be Repeated

MANY THINGS MADE THE summer of 1956 a special summer for Hammad, with its radiant atmosphere and optimistic memories. The declaration of Moroccan independence in March 1956 had begun to be implemented and he had passed the tawjihiya (baccalaureate). Then came the announcement of the nationalization of the Suez Canal in July to crown these events and determine their path.

Hammad was not in Morocco at independence but he and his friends were in Port Said when Gamal Abd al-Nasser announced the nationalization of the Suez Canal in Manshiya Square in Alexandria. However, being part of or close to an event does not mean that we grasp all its dimensions and unexpected consequences. With hindsight we can analyze, criticize, or defend it, but it isn't the same event as the one we watched unfold, when we were taken by surprise and when something that we had wished for or only imagined took place. Maybe our lives are simply a limited set of events that we experience in our personal lives or in the public sphere with others. But even a public event only acquires its character when it is particularized in one's memory, through details, scenes, and words, which transform it into a kind of pearl that rises in the middle of the darkness and stirs, in the slumbering depths, the process of remembrance and recreation of the period that accompanied it.

Hammad and a group of friends who were not returning to Morocco for the holiday decided to go to Port Said for two weeks to explore the then small town and renew their bond with the sea, as they would back home during the summer. They spent a week immersed in the coast and its enjoyable scenes, wandering about the town and visiting small fish restaurants, surrendering to relaxation after a year of hard work. On the morning of July 26 there was unusual activity in the town. Everyone was talking about an important event that Nasser would announce in his speech to the nation that evening. They eagerly prepared themselves to listen to his enchanting and captivating voice. One of them suggested that they listen from the harbor, where a large platform had been erected with loudspeakers to transmit the speech over the airwaves with all the important politicians assembled. It was nine o'clock, as the night yielded to the sea breezes and silence reigned over the crowd gathered around the platform and microphones, when the voice of Nasser—penetrating, gripping, mocking, challenging, and sincere—rang out with that spontaneity which aimed straight at people's emotions. Hearts surrendered to the rhythmic waves and magical tone, and blazed as he articulated deeply buried sentiments. Throats burned as they cheered the hero who raised the country's head high. They listened to the speech intoxicated, their bodies electrified. Hammad studied the faces in the crowd and their reactions and pride at the decision to nationalize the canal. Nasser talked and reiterated and the people were captivated.

Could the same effect and fascination take hold without his special narrative, constructed of details, scenes, statistics, excitement, mockery, and emotive language? To what extent did the people, or rather peoples, really pay attention to the particulars as they beheld this man filling the void of inactivity that afflicted their history and memory? They eagerly soaked up the words of the brown-skinned hero who ventured to mend the rips, bandage the wounds, and construct a narrative of reform in a loud voice for all to hear. When Hammad recalled the episode in its proper time and context, the distance he later acquired—when he read about the events and understood Nasser's role in creating, fashioning, and exploiting them—evaporated. The man was, as many said, like an affectionate father guiding an orphaned tribe that had been oppressed by evil administrators. Hammad had felt, though remotely and without really being conscious of it at the time, that Nasser was inaugurating a new phase, which had been a long time coming and whose slogan was that Egypt and the Arabs would have the courage from that day forth, from the day that Suez was nationalized, to participate directly in constructing their own history. The goal was clear, the will to defend it steadfast, and the expression eloquent and captivating. Thus Hammad was not able to get away from the halo that surrounded the image of Nasser in his memory, especially when he pictured him in the middle of the crowd in Azhar Square after the Tripartite Assault was announced, or when he listened to him addressing Cairo University after the declaration of the United Arab Republic, or when he saw him at close quarters at the summit in Casablanca in 1965. In Hammad's imagination Nasser was not a creature of flesh and blood but a vital force who filled the vacuum and swept all else aside with his words and opinions. His presence had an overwhelming power.

On the night the Suez Canal was nationalized, the hanging about on the seafront and wandering through the happy sleepless town continued until late. When Hammad and his friends returned to the small hostel, where they were renting a large room with seven beds, they found a new Moroccan student, who had just arrived by steamer from Syria, where he had been studying. The student was older than them, tall, and had a loud voice and thick spectacles. He had spent three years in Damascus but, for reasons that weren't clear, had decided to come to Cairo to finish his studies. The evening stretched on and the student with the loud voice spoke at length, analyzing, commenting on, and commending nationalization and its hero. His lexicon was distinguished by words and phrases from the Baath Party, as Hammad would discover in the following year. Thus the events of that day were inextricably linked, in Hammad's mind, to this loud-voiced student with his exuberant chatter and conviction that from now on the doors were open for the Arabs under Egypt's leadership. He went on at great length, delighted to talk for Hammad and his friends, who were desperately sleepy. One of them suddenly got up and turned out the light but the student with the loud voice chatted on, twisting and kneading his words for their benefit.

In the run-up to the tawjihiya in May, the North African Student Lodge in Agouza was a hive of activity, trampled by students as they revised their lessons, studied their curriculum books, and, from time to time, traded explanations, questions, and humorous remarks. Their faces were unshaven and most of them were in striped pajamas. They would send the doorman, Amm Uthman, to fetch them tea. There were slightly more students from Morocco than Algeria or Tunisia. Among the Moroccans there were two distinct blocks: the North Moroccans, who assembled around the poet and storyteller Salil al-Sharafa, a self-important guy who acted as their leader, and the Moroccans from the south, who mostly belonged to, or sympathized with, the Independence Party. There wasn't open confrontation between the two groups but there was a kind of rivalry, nourished by pride at belonging to the region that produced Muhammad bin Abd al-Karim al-Khattabi and the magical words of the major poet Yara. Gradually, a stirring poem composed by Yara became an anthem for the North Moroccan students. They would sing it exuberantly and gaily at communal evening gatherings: "Oh France, Get ready. . . ."

In mocking reaction the students from the south elected the thickset Abd al-Rahman al-Fakiki, who did a good impression of Nasser, as their leader. They would shout his name and demand rousing phrases. The poor guy was lost between believing the 'pledge of allegiance' and suspecting the evil intentions of his friends. Nevertheless, he would spend hours memorizing Nasser's speeches and practicing their delivery. In any case, the 'leader' al-Fakiki was good at playing the role of satirical imitator, a role that tempered the ambitions of leadership founded on legs of clay.

After the tawjihiya was over and the results published, and it was confirmed that the grant from independent Morocco was on its way, preparations to leave or to find apartments began. Hammad was surprised by his friend Nabih's decision to travel to France after a successful year at the College of Law. There was only a short time left for the two of them to amuse themselves, in the evening in cafes and restaurants and during the day by going to the Metro cinema to be refreshed by its air-conditioner and new American film; like *Some Like It Hot* (Marilyn Monroe), *Tea and Sympathy* (Deborah Kerr), and *Separate Tables* (Deborah Kerr).

That summer Hammad also began going to the Raphaeli and Opera Complex cinemas to watch Egyptian films, especially when the stars attended the first showing: Faten Hamama, Farid al-Atrash, Farid Shawqi, Shadya, Mahmoud al-Meligi. . . . The shouting, cheering, and clapping began as soon as the hero or heroine arrived. Sometimes the hero would be carried on the crowd's shoulders. The spectators would jostle together and voices would cheer the actors and actresses throughout the show.

The intoxication of nationalization lasted for a few weeks. On the streets, in houses, on the radio, and in the newspapers everyone was talking about "the master's slap," which knocked the breath out of those with shares and interests in the canal and announced the birth of a new man of action who did not drift along with the wishes of the exploiters. But the clouds soon thickened, warning that the West would not take lightly the blow that shook it so thoroughly. At the same time, the event gained momentum and took on its proper vast proportions, indicating a new turn in the relationship with yesterday's colonizers, who had appointed themselves eternal overlords. The impact was greater than the effect of a rock falling into a stagnant bog. Indeed it was an event that continued to produce repercussions and confrontation.

Then came the inevitable: the Israeli attack of October 29 and the Tripartite Assault (after France and England joined forces on November 5), which burst out from Port Said to reclaim the nationalized canal. But what the foreigners really wanted was to punish the brown-skinned hero and his companions, who dared to rebel and break the exploitative agreements.

Hammad and his friends were excited and proud to be witnessing glorious and defining moments close up and felt a deep affinity with Arab destiny as it faced a difficult test in pioneering Egypt. At the North African Student Club several meetings were held to express support and to volunteer, along with the other Arab students, in defending the Suez Canal. But the days were not devoid of cheer and novelty despite the drums sounding for war.

After registering their names they were assigned a day to go to one of the army bases in Cairo for weapons training.

"Is this the only time we'll receive weapons training?" asked one of them.

"So what? Do you think this is a game? You're volunteering your blood and soul. If you die you'll be a martyr. Lucky you!"

They were in their final days at the North African Lodge and their collective discussions and comments were growing more enthusiastic, while they made light of the dangers.

After the weapons training their fear of guns and bullets eased a little. Anthems and zealous songs filled Cairo's open spaces and stuck in people's heads for tongues to repeat, especially one song: "I left my weapons for a time / Now I can't wait for battle." The day after the training they were told to go to a school in Doqqi at sunset to receive overnight training in defending the city quarters, spreading the watchword, "Turn out the lights" when the warning siren was heard, and ambushing Israeli, French, and British soldiers, who had taken it upon themselves to descend by parachute into the streets of Cairo.

They arrived at the school in Doqqi in groups and were met by Corporal Abul Ela and his deputy Abul Futuh, who were dressed in khaki army uniforms with pistols on their hips. They were both around thirty and their faces looked stern and serious. After welcoming and thanking them they switched to a tone of command and emphasized the need to obey orders precisely. They would sleep at the school but right now must go out in double-file around the quarters of Doqqi and practice informing residents to turn out the lights as a precaution against air raids.

There were about thirty students and the circuit alternated between walking and jogging. It stretched on and some of them began to sweat badly. When it was dark, the corporal stopped them under a building in al-Masaha. "Attention." "Right," he shouted, "Abul Futuh will blow the whistle and you'll spread out around the buildings and villas and shout 'Turn off the lights.' Attention. Quiet."

Abul Futuh blew the whistle loudly and they began rushing around and shouting, laughing enough to be heard: "Turn off the lights. You there on the second floor . . . we're practicing for an air raid. Obey orders."

A group of students began to divide the command into two parts and each band took over shouting one of them. "Turn off," called the first. "The lights," the second cut in. "Turn off . . . . The lights . . . . The lights . . . . Turn off . . . ."

"Stop laughing," Abul Ela bellowed sternly. "This is serious. Attention! Quick. Gather round me. Right here."

Hours went by and the training still wasn't over. "I'm sure he brought us here so he can show off his muscles to a girl he's after who lives round here," said one student.

It was nearly ten o'clock when they returned to the school in Doqqi. They were surprised not to find any supper, only tea; they could buy food and snacks from the grocery. They asked where they would sleep. "Here in these classrooms," said Abul Ela. "We in a state of war, effendis. Tonight is vital training for you."

They did not follow this logic and began arguing and object-ing. As long as we have finished training for the night we can return to the North African Lodge and come back in the morn-ing, said some of them. Abul Ela protested that he had been instructed not to leave them and to talk to them about the rules of popular resistance so they could be sent off to guard posts with rifles the next day. He even whetted their appetites and ignited their emotions by saying, "You know, we made a pledge, me and my friend Abul Futuh, when we volunteered in the popular resistance—whether we live or die." They applauded him for a long time then carried on trying to con-vince him that sleeping on tables and desks, with no blankets and covers, was unfeasible and would make them heavy in the morning. At that Abul Ela said enthusiastically, "How about we go to the North African Lodge and get some blankets?" Everyone shouted their agreement, thinking to themselves that once they got there they would not leave but convince him and

Abul Futuh to stay with them in the common room. Which is exactly what happened!

In the warm Cairo autumn sun, the Moroccan students were distributed to guard posts in Agouza and Doqqi. They were handed unloaded rifles (the bullets, they were told, would be given out later) and instructed to keep their eyes on the sky and watch for enemy planes, and to patrol the stretch assigned to their post constantly. The corporal and his deputy would be coming round to inspect. Whenever Hammad tried to visualize those moments he couldn't picture himself carrying a rifle on his skinny shoulder. He was thin in those days and his face had not yet lost its child-like freshness, despite the mustache he had grown in the Egyptian manner after passing the tawjihiya. But the scene of that first day of guard duty remained etched in his memory because of one particular event, which still made his friends laugh whenever they recalled it.

The autumn sun was shining softly and Hammad was on the Nile Corniche in Agouza, dressed in a short-sleeved shirt, carrying an unloaded rifle, and making his way up the street with orderly steps until he reached the guard post of a friend, who was waiting to chat and look up at the sky with him, which appeared completely clear and showed not the slightest sign of an air raid. Over three hours went by, it was past one o'clock, and hunger pangs began to make themselves known. They had not been told anything about meals or when the guard duty would end. After being patient for a little, Hammad told himself that there was no harm in buying something to curb his hunger, especially as "the front" seemed quiet. He headed to the nearest grocery and bought cheese, sweetmeats, bread, and black olives, then returned to his guard spot and selected the step of a building to have his lunch and continue watching the sky. He spread his food out on a palm-stalk mat and began chewing and swallowing with relish. His head moved between the food and the sky alternately, ignoring the passersby. After a little while he felt two tall figures obstruct his vision. He looked up carefully. There was Corporal Abul Ela and his deputy Abul Futuh gazing at him suspiciously and sternly. He stood up, gathering up his rifle, which was beside him, and quickly performed the military salute with his left hand.

"What's this, Ustaz? Saluting with your left hand?" Abul Ela bellowed at him.

Hammad transferred his rifle from his right shoulder to his left and raised his right hand, correcting his salute.

"Good God. Leaving guard duty and sitting down for lunch? You haven't respected the instructions we gave you. No, no, it's not good enough."

Abul Futuh intervened, "It's okay this time, bey, but any more slips will be punished."

Hammad was ashamed and embarrassed, especially as some children and pedestrians and the doorman of the building were watching the scene and heard his reprimand. But after the two men left he laughed at himself and the muddle that made him forget what he had been taught at the rapid "military training."

The summer of 1956 ended with the Tripartite Assault, which did not achieve its objectives but instead ignited a blaze of resistance among the Egyptian people and inaugurated a new phase in the history of liberation and in the Arabs' control of their destiny. Nasser's speech at the Azhar Mosque confirmed this new birth. When Hammad recalled that summer, he found that it stood out in his memory. Despite the fears and reservations that he and his friends heard voiced at the house of the leader Allal al-Fassi, Morocco's independence was the threshold to a new era. Hammad was happy because his friend Fatah, who had been given the death sentence by the French when he was sixteen, could regain his freedom, having escaped from Kenitra Prison before independence and been living in hiding in plantations and small villages ever since. They had been together at secondary school. After the king was detained, he and some other pupils had set up a guerrilla cell in Rabat, which carried out a number of operations before it was apprehended. The cell announced the dawn of a new generation within the framework of the party that sowed the first seeds of consciousness, seeds that would soon embrace the language of violence to speed up the hour of liberation.

Hammad's success in the baccalaureate brought him closer to following the path that he had dreamed of since the first year of secondary school: to study literature and become a writer, gathering up the feelings, moments, and ideas that hovered dimly in his soul and the souls of his friends and countrymen at the time. Perhaps this yearning originated early in his childhood in Fez as he listened to stories from the *Arabian Nights* read by a friend of his uncle at chaste evening gatherings, or when he began to discover the stories of Kamil Kilani. But the tendency toward literature, notwithstanding the broadness of the term, took root and intensified during secondary school, when he became acquainted with the writings of al-Manfaluti, Gibran, Taha Hussein, Tawfiq al-Hakim, and Jurji Zaydan. These writings bred in him a fascination for distant Egypt, which he envisaged to be like a box of wonders from which sprang all that captivated the imagination of children and adults: films, songs, stories, and texts that restored Arabic literature's splendor and ability to influence. He sometimes supposed that it was his love of literature and his writing aspirations that kept him going on his little adventure of traveling to Egypt and deceiving the French administration. Thus the summer of 1956 was not simply the next step on the road but an event that inaugurated a phase, which was distinguished by its very nature from the world that Hammad was used to. When he tried to philosophize his relationship with that phase and that exceptional summer, he would recall what he had read about the "Big Bang," which physicists and modern astronomers regarded

32

as the beginning of the earth's existence, the moment it split off from the other parts of the universe. It was as though, since his journey from Rabat to Cairo through France and Italy, Hammad had been heading toward a "big bang," whose characteristics only began to crystalize in the summer of '56, when he became aware that his being had separated from its former orbit and was entering a second beginning in his life. His childhood beginnings seemed separate from the realm of this second beginning, with its intermeshed boundaries, for it no longer pointed from the present to the future through ascending linear time; rather it was the beginning of a journey that was not oriented toward events so much as it responded to the needs of the cell tissue of his new memory, which was penetrating further and further into different spaces and labyrinths of anxious questions about belonging, being, and carnal desire. Later, in a pensive moment, Hammad thought to himself: this second beginning came about because of his attraction to the Egyptian dialect, which abounded with magic and metaphors and was capable of laying hold of everyday life through quick, incisive expressions. Was not every different dialect and language part of an existence that we annex to our lives?

Perhaps the secret wager that directed Hammad's first steps was formed early on, amid that flood of activity that sought to reclaim the impounded homeland by repossessing the language that soldered its people's memories. Next to the powerful French language and its adroit transfigurations, Arabic relied on the glories of the past and on a living memory that produced dialect to translate emotion. Was it true that repossessing the homeland meant inhabiting a language capable of expressing the constituents and mutations of identity? That is, by inhabiting a language, entering the land and the spaces to which we belong? The argument involved a degree of mythologizing but it ignited Hammad's craving to write when he was small and his receptiveness to the Egyptian dialect, with its capacity to expand and embody thanks to expressive possibilities that grasped daily life and broadened the Arabic language. As Hammad practiced idioms and new expressions, he began to realize that he was learning to inhabit a wider terrain than simply a land imbued with a language that exuded a special pagan beauty and was colored by the desert sands before the dawn of Islam opened the doors to other languages.

Hammad recalled being utterly amazed by the ruins of ancient Egypt, especially on a school trip to Luxor and Aswan in the spring of 1956. The train was full of students from the Husayniya School. Anthems, songs, shouting, and laughter resounded and everyone was sucking sugar cane, which they had bought at one of the stations on the long journey. When Hammad visited the Sphinx and the Pyramids at Giza after arriving in Cairo, he remembered a poem by Ahmad Shawqi that he had memorized in the third year of secondary school, without knowing at the time that this beautiful history struck its roots deep in the land of Egypt and its memory. His amazement was greatest in Luxor, exploring the temples of Karnak, its giant pillars, speaking statues, and inscriptions on the towering obelisks. A sort of bewilderment overcame him as he studied the harmonious distillation of mummies, animals, and ornaments beneath the moon and sun. At the time he did not pay much attention to the commentaries around him but sensed the place was different to other ruins he had seen. His senses were overcome by the beauty of the faces, inscriptions, and colors. He was equally bewildered when he visited the Valleys of the Kings and Queens on the west bank of the Nile, where the noble pharaohs built their splendid tombs, crammed full of precious objects and rare curiosities. Pitchers, long-necked bottles, pipes, gold vessels, cups, large plates. . . . Many years later, reading *The Book of the Dead*, he felt the overwhelming presence of the mummies, pharaonic obelisks, gods, priests, scribes, and servant girls woven intimately with the world of the Hereafter, whose inhabitants remain with us through the outer shapes, rituals, and symbols that represent their ongoing life on the banks of the Nile from Heliopolis and Wadi Natrun to Philae Island and Abu Simbel.

At the end of 1996, on board a boat from Luxor to Aswan, Hammad had the opportunity to contemplate the specters and figures that touched his imagination in 1956. He paused at the Ramesseum or "Palace of a Million Years," which Ramesses II built for the god Amon and himself as a vast tomb and filled with grand edifices, pillars, tunnels, and statues, and pondered the elegant movements of the offering-bearers, dancers, and musicians, the fishermen and women, the lotus flowers, and the crocodiles, lions, vipers, scarabs, and goat-headed creatures. He wondered for a long time: was the powerful presence of the statues of ancient Egyptian civilization and the intimacy they bred to do with the fact that the ancient Egyptians did not see death as an ending and therefore strove to save the body from decay, so it would be easier for the soul to reclaim it in the Hereafter or a potential second life on earth? Or was the source of this intimacy that the artistic expression of these symbols and religious rituals far exceeded the priests' intentions and kings' ambitions for eternal life? The rulers' purpose in building the Pyramids and the vast burial chambers, sarcophagi, statues, inscriptions, vessels, and mummies had disappeared but the beauty produced by the hands and imaginations of the artists, whose names ancient Egyptian art did not preserve, just as it didn't the anonymous authors and scribes who composed the books of law, ethics, and funeral texts, survived. Those who believe in the possibility of correspondence between art and reality would say that the power of these treasures exists in their "concrete" representation of the life of the pharaohs, important men, and daily existence. But this limited interpretation ignores the dreams and aspirations of the artists who constructed a vision that cranes its neck from over five thousand years ago to beyond the earth's horizon, to lengthen the "eye of the sun" and stir people to look beyond reality. Some Egyptian tablets record the dreams of kings and queens. There were priests who specialized in their interpretation and their law books confirmed that "the lord creates dreams in order to make the path clear for mankind, since he cannot see the future." So pharaonic art could be seen as a dream striving to take its place among other dreams of the future. It was art that mingled the bodies of humans and animals with mixtures of plants, clay, and stone, clear colors and the sun's reflections on the pillars of temples and obelisks. It seemed to say to us, "Men are just characters in one of God's dreams."

"How great is the dream that creates and is able to bring back the ecstasy of being created and the illusion of perfection!"

In Aswan, Hammad saw the Nile flowing in torrents, swelling like a raging sea, surrounded by plains, fields, thickets, dry clay rocks, and the froth of the surging river as it followed its course southward. It was as though, in this encounter full of pictures from a beautiful, refined civilization, his memory was striving to take in the treasure, which was new for him, having never set eyes on it before. As he gazed at the temples, statues, inscriptions, and obelisks, he understood that his journey to Egypt was more than an endeavor to complete a picture of which he knew some features; it was a journey into the unknown, whose return to presence brought with it essential questions, first formulated by man as he walked the banks of the Nile at the dawn of history.

Nothing is pre-given. As we approach what we thought was truth we discover new dimensions, embodying phenomena and problems we ignored when we formed our questions in the first place. Memory, too, is far from unified; it too is like the summer of 1956, which would never be repeated in Hammad's life. Or, more precisely, memory is plural in terms of homeland and space. Thus we live between two fires, as they say: the utopia of memory and the utopia of desire. Whenever we remember, desire creeps in to color our memory, and whenever we surrender to desire we make it draw on some paradisiacal memory.

University

HAMMAD GOT TO KNOW the gate of Cairo University, its tall dome, and the chimes of its famous clock on his way to the zoological gardens. He waited longingly for the end of the summer so that he could enter the complex, which symbolized a dream he had entertained since he was a schoolboy in Rabat. He and Barhum had inquired about the names of the teachers, first-year curriculum, and teaching methods, and began preparing for this next difficult stage after they passed the tawjihiya.

The first few weeks were characterized by excitement and eagerness to attend every lecture and visit the library regularly to read reference books. The process of getting to know other students was slow as there was no occasion designed to facilitate it. Hammad and Barhum noticed that the level of beauty among the female students was below average, or approached it with difficulty. There were students from Egypt, Saudi, Jordan, Syria, and Malaysia but communication was almost nonexistent. Each person was like an island. The teaching method of most teachers did not permit students to participate in the discussion or present their thoughts. Hammad remembered how Dr. Shawqi Daif would spend the whole period dictating his lectures on the history of literature, so in the winter term Barhum stopped attending this elementary class and asked Hammad to take notes for him.

Later on, in the third year, the students agreed to ask Dr. Shawqi to set time aside for questions and discussion. He listened to their request, took off his spectacles, was silent for a while, then said that his dictation was the essential foundation and it was up to them to go to the sources and references if they wanted more. As for discussion, it was pointless at this level. He replaced his spectacles and continued dictating. Nevertheless, most students approved of dictation and relied on rote learning to guarantee success. This was the principle followed by the majority of teachers, with the exception of Suhayr al-Qalamawi, Abd al-Hamid Yunus, Shukri Ayyad, and Dr. Ibrahim Hammouda, who taught Qur'an rhetoric and informed the students that he would alternate between dictation and explanation and that they must distinguish between the two processes through the change in his voice. Sometimes he would notice students continuing to write when he was explaining. "Are you writing?" he would shout. "Didn't you notice the change in my tone of voice? Are you an idiot?"

The syllabi were long and their contents did not cover the relationship between literature and life that Hammad and Barhum, who were endeavoring to write short stories and poetry, had hoped to explore. They realized that what concerned them and what they were striving for lay outside the Arabic Language and Literature Department. It was a realm that could be entered via the cafeteria of the College of Arts, where a group of journalists, young writers, and, in particular, beautiful female students from the Sociology or French Literature Departments, would meet. Here leaders from all over the Arab world would come alive and debate, and occasionally literary and art get-togethers were organized to which rising names of the day were invited. Hammad remembered listening to Salah Abd al-Sabbour reciting his poem "I Shall Kill You," which was inspired by the Tripartite Aggression. Here too the talents of the singer Safinaz Kazem, who would perform songs by Fayrouz, were unveiled. Just as the Arabic Language Department was surrounded by an aura of gravity and high "academic" standards, so the cafeteria of the College of Arts teemed with rebellious voices, questioning and plunging headlong into politics and writing projects. The North African Students' Club was another window onto the literary and intellectual scene in Cairo. Its organizing committee invited Ahmad Abd al-Muti Hijazi to recite poems from *City without a Heart* and the young critic Ragaa al-Naqqash to deliver a lecture on new criticism. The apartment opposite the North African Students' Club was the site of the Modern Egyptian Writers Association, whose president was the late Mustafa al-Sihrati. There Hammad met Naguib Surour, who had returned from the Soviet Union, and invited him to play a game of table tennis.

The College of Arts occupied a special place in Hammad's heart. He greatly enjoyed the lectures of Dr. Yusuf Khalif, as he breathed life into pre-Islamic poetry and unveiled the finesse of Abbasid verse. Through the voice of Abd al-Hamid Yunus he became acquainted with issues of creativity and its relation to the soul, memory, and senses. Suhayr al-Qalamawi motivated students to enter the field of criticism in its deep sense, combining theoretical aspects with what manifested in texts themselves. In the fourth year, there was a twice-monthly encounter with Taha Hussein, with his captivating, musical delivery, selected classical expressions, and steady, heart-rending voice. However, it was their private lessons with Sayyida Nadia, the French language and literature teacher, that most delighted Hammad and his friend Barhum, for no one else had chosen the language of Racine as their second language. The source of enjoyment in these classes was that the teacher, once she was acquainted with them and their literary interests, would consult them when selecting texts for reading and analysis and topics from literary history. These classes gave Hammad and his friend the opportunity to connect directly with Sartre, Camus, Mauriac, and André Gide, the names circling the French skies and enjoying particular appreciation among the vanguard of Arab critics at the time, after some of their novels had been translated. The French class was thus an opportunity to learn grammar and practice speaking, as well as a space in which to study a different kind of literary writing, which in turn opened the way to voice apprehensions and inner feelings and to plunge into the depths of being. Such opportunities were not granted in the Arabic Language Department, where literature came to a halt with Hafiz Ibrahim and Ahmad Shawqi. In the second year, a female student with a degree in French literature, who wanted to study Arabic language and literature in order to undertake some literary research, joined the department. Susan was completely different to the other female students. She spoke naturally with everyone, had a curiosity for knowledge, and a propensity for laughter and fun. Perhaps it was these characteristics, rather than their interest in French, that brought Hammad, Barhum, and Susan together in a kind of threesome that spent the free time between classes joking, watching students and teachers' slip-ups, as well as discussing literature, books, and the contents of various magazines and studies. Susan was the best at French and would show them what to read and select classes for them to attend in the French Literature Department, where Dr. Munis Hussein taught. They were much obliged, especially as they found the girls studying French literature attractive, with their striking beauty and elegance. There they became acquainted with Wahid, who had green eyes, a bright face, and shy smile. Wahid had experimented with writing and had refined artistic tastes. They would meet, together with Susan, in the cafeteria to laugh and exchange news and opinions. As the days passed, Hammad and Barhum observed (whether it was the case or they were just imagining it) that Wahid was imbued with the conversation of their friend and barely took his eyes off her, despite his evident shyness. His conversation at times created the impression of "a mighty army of desire" in his heart. But the wind didn't blow to where the ship of the beloved was headed, and she seemed unaware of his silent adoration.

When Hammad met Wahid in Paris in 1971, he was married with children, but his amiability, shyness, and appetite for knowledge remained. He was preparing a thesis on Egyptian theater and had published some fine stories in magazines, translated a book from French, and was generally highly thought of. Perhaps Barhum and I imagined his lonely love story, Hammad thought to himself. But the deep sorrow in Wahid's green eyes and in his stories betrayed a hidden wound that would stay with him from the prime of his youth to the end of his life.

Hammad and Barhum were friendly with some of the Egyptian students but it did not really go beyond curriculum interests and rivalry in exams and research, probably because they didn't share the same writing aspirations. One of them was Munim, an industrious student who was eager to excel, whereas Hammad and Barhum wanted to do well but without neglecting what was going on outside the university. As time went by, a group formed of six or seven top students who impressed the teachers. Though they competed among themselves, they found themselves scheming together in the fourth year against a teacher who had been asked to teach them modern literary criticism when it was not his field. The teacher entered the first class and talked about the subjects they would be dealing with, namely the relationship between literature and society, commitment and its theory, and the relavance of some contemporary criticism for Arabic literature. He spoke generally and pompously, but before long was asking the class for its views on the relationship between literature and commitment. It was a good opportunity for the top students to display their knowledge and superiority over the others. Each of them raised his hand to set forth the viewpoints of Sartre, Taha Hussein, and the scholar Mahmoud Amin, while the teacher made do with nodding his head and uttering, "Not bad." When the six students had finished their expositions, the teacher began to arrange and structure what they had said, without adding anything. When the class was over they looked at one another and smiled, having realized that the teacher wanted to conduct his lectures on their backs under the pretence of complying with their wish for discussion and debate. They agreed to avoid the trap of tempting questions in the next class, so the teacher got into a fix, as they say.

Hammad's relationship with the cinema grew stronger in Cairo while studying at the university. He had first discovered it in Fez as a child of six or seven, when he would go with his cousin to the cinema in Bab Boujeloud to watch Egyptian films like *Long Live Love*, *Forbidden Love*, *Love and Revenge*, and *Antar and Abla*, as well as American westerns. But in Cairo he discovered other kinds of films, which were full of love and sex scenes and came with an Arabic translation, for example, films like *Tea and Sympathy*, *Separate Tables*, *Some Like It Hot*, and *The Man With the Golden Arm*, and actors and actresses like Deborah Kerr, Grace Kelly, Marilyn Monroe, Glenn Ford, James Stewart, and Frank Sinatra. From May onward, Cairo began to get very hot and the air-conditioned Metro Cinema would draw in Hammad and his friend from ten in the morning, possibly to return for the half past two showing, while they waited for the Nile's evening breeze. Some Egyptian films attracted their curiosity, especially as the heroes and heroines would attend the first showing amid a lot of noise and excitement. Hammad remembered going with some Egyptian friends to watch a film starring Farid al-Atrash and Iman when they were in the audience and being astonished by the crowd's warm reception and cheering. His friends explained that film producers and film stars always hired a group of people, known as 'the hatifa,' with the specific job of praising, clapping, and beating drums, who, throughout the film, cheered the main actor and actress and vilified their enemies. That evening the noise was loud in the hall. When there was a moment of quiet, people would call out, "Farid, envy of all," or "You heartthrob" when he sang in his lachrymose voice with tears streaming.

Hammad also remembered, as part of his adventures outside university, the first performance he attended, with his friend Abduh, of Umm Kulthum in 1957, when she sang "Whom Should I Go To?" for the first time. He was astounded by the crowd's delight, the ritual of listening and savoring, and all the moaning. He recalled someone in the audience in a peasant gallabiya with a cotton skullcap on his head and white shawl around his neck rushing from the back of the hall to near the front of the stage, bowing, and shouting, "From the beginning again, Sayyida. From the beginning, I kiss your hands," requesting a section that particularly delighted him to be repeated. There was clapping and the lady smiled and signaled with her finger to Abduh Salih, the qanun player, to play it again.

The year before, Hammad and Barhum had discovered the Tawfiqiya Coffeeshop, which was dedicated to fans of Umm Kulthum. It was a scene of swaying heads, voices singing along, chests sighing, cigarettes and roll-ups, cups of tea, coffee, salep and karkadeh, domino matches, and waiters shouting out customers' orders and repeat orders. They preferred to come in the evening and ascend to the next floor, where the lights would be turned out, except for what crept in through the windows, and admirers would listen humbly or moan in amorous rapture, clutching the mouthpieces of narghiles which fanned the fires of their desire. "How I'm wronged," a wounded voice would come out of the corner of the dark hall, "Oh madam, yes, I accept I'm wronged." "Your acceptance is an illusion. I dream of you until bereft of sleep," sang the overwhelming voice. "Oh lady, bereft. . . ." However the ecstasy of listening did not fill the gap that sometimes opened up between Hammad and the scene of these sad afflicted men, stupefied by the range of this voice that flitted between loud and soft. He tried to comprehend the deprivation that these melancholy faces exuded. He compared the affection he saw between couples and lovers in the gardens and streets of France with the exclusively male retreat of the Tawfiqiya Coffeeshop, where there was an apparition of the hoped-for beloved but no physical or human presence. He had been amazed, since his arrival in Cairo, to see women at the heart of the family as well as able to move about freely in other spheres. He realized that there was a huge difference in the presence of women in Egypt and absence of women in Morocco, though he still couldn't stomach the men's surrender to sadness which exaggerated sentiments he used to think natural and easy. When he discussed this with Barhum, his friend told him that he had not yet experienced anything that set his ardent heart alight and that his fleeting adventures did not enter the category of love and its derivatives. Hammad was accustomed to his friend the poet telling him every now and then that it did not take more than four months for a relationship with a Moroccan or Egyptian student to progress beyond romantic caresses and stroking. These relationships were indispensable for Barhum to write his poems and were what convinced Hammad to accompany him to the Tawfiqiya Coffeeshop in the first place. In the third year of university, Barhum progressed from the phase of romance with female students to the phase of reality and what followed.

Uncharacteristically, he began attending every class, including eight o'clock ones, taking notes during lectures and buying printed lectures. "At last it's my turn to have a break from following the teachers' dictations!" said Hammad. But Barhum smiled and explained that he was only responding to the request of a female colleague who could not attend regularly.

"Who's the lucky girl?" "Mufida, the Lebanese girl I introduced you to last week. She teaches in Sidon and can only attend some weeks." "Oh, Mufida." Hammad recalled that she had tanned skin and a good figure but her features were coarse and her skin and face dull and rather pallid, and she seemed shy or introverted. Never mind, Hammad said to himself; perhaps the lectures in Arab nationalism, which were delivered to all university students without exception, had borne fruit, for Barhum was beginning to enact the solidarity and unity in concrete form! One evening in December, Barhum returned to the apartment in a state, trembling from the cold and something else. Hammad looked at him and Barhum burst out laughing as he threw himself down on the chair and breathed a sigh of relief. It was an unusual story. Barhum had invited Mufida to Qasr al-Nil Casino and sensed she was interested so thought a little and suggested that they take a walk along the bank of the Nile under the bridge. They held hands and, as dark crept in, their bodies got closer and they stole a kiss. He deliberated and, having noted that the shore was empty of people that cold night, they advanced further under the bridge to the bough of a tree with a thick trunk. There their bodies came together, standing upright, and progressed beyond the kissing stage. But their movements and the blood in their veins froze when they heard the steps of the sergeant patrolling the bridge above them. They moved closer together, as though both wanting to sink into the tree trunk, and hardly breathed as they waited for the officer's footsteps to pass. It seemed like a long time and their bodies trembled from everything; the pleasure, the cold, and the fear. Once the sergeant was gone they slipped off, buttoning up their clothes. Hammad laughed a lot as he listened to the 'standing' adventure. He fetched two cups and a bottle of brandy to warm his friend and drink a toast to escaping the bridge predicament. "Getting to know Mufida worked out well. Lucky you," he said to him.

◎

Some Friday mornings would see unusual commotion in the flat, when Hammad, Barhum, and Alaa were getting up early and preparing to go to Abbas Mahmoud al-Aqqad's house in Heliopolis. Their friend Darnkali, who studied philosophy with Alaa, would come along too. It was probably his idea in the first place, for he told them one day how he had been in the Anglo-Egyptian Bookshop with the Moroccan newspaper *al-'Ilm*, which contained poems celebrating the coronation, in his hand and seen Ustaz al-Aqqad sitting in a corner. He ventured to greet him and introduce himself, and express his admiration for his work. Al-Aqqad noticed the newspaper, took it, and thumbed through. When he found the last page was given entirely to a columnar poem, he smiled and said, "You lot in Morocco are still writing traditional poems!" Darnkali loved relating this anecdote, his loud laughter declaring his contempt for what he saw as Morocco's cultural backwardness. On their first visit, Hammad was full of apprehension as al-Aqqad's name was always accompanied by "the great writer" and because his language was subtle and his subjects diverse, and Hammad sometimes found them difficult. Stories about al-Aqqad portrayed him as a giant with a vicious tongue and strong personality. The apartment was in an ordinary building and books lined the entrance, hall, and small reception room, which was filled with young and middle-aged men. Al-Aqqad sat in his pajamas with a white cotton skullcap on his head. He stood up to welcome them and people began spreading out to make space for the Moroccan students to sit. Al-Aqqad resumed talking, putting his hands inside the waistband of his pajama trousers, completely at ease, as though he was sitting alone. After a short while a servant came in carrying glasses of lemonade. Hammad recalled a group of faces he would see there whenever he visited. Their owners were like disciples, for they would learn by heart extracts of al-Aqqad's articles and poems and often interrupt to complete what he was referring to. Hence one of them might say, "As you wrote in your article in the journal *al-Hilal* in 1932, where you said . . . ." and begin quoting an entire section that al-Aqqad had written twenty years earlier. Hammad was astonished at the ease with which al-Aqqad moved from literature and history to issues of agriculture, medicine, and physics, analyzing and citing titles of books and studies published in English. He spoke in a hoarse voice and laughed loudly when he told a joke or funny story, or when he shot a biting remark at an opponent. Once he commented on someone who had written an article mocking his romanticism in *Sarah* and insulting his virility: "If they go and ask the doorman of my old building he'll tell them about all the girls who visited me, one arriving as the other left." On most visits, Hammad and his friends found the critic Muhammad Tahir al-Gabalawi and the Tunisian Muhammad Khalifa. Once the poet Abd al-Rahman Sidqi, with his tall frame and remarkable elegance, was there, and another time the short story writer Jadhibiya Sidqi came, though women rarely attended. The Friday visit was an opportunity for Egyptian and Arab writers to bring samples of their work to the great writer. Hammad remembered that al-Aqqad was very critical of communism and those who rallied under its banner. When a journalist questioned him about it he replied, "It's because I love democracy with all its faults. I prefer it to communism even if the latter has merits." Hammad could not remember the contents of what was said at these sessions, but he recalled the special atmosphere that emanated from the group gathered around al-Aqqad, talking, laughing, and mocking, relaxed in his nightclothes, free of affectation and constraint. Perhaps it was this that made his visitors feel familiar and at ease and enjoy agreeing with his likes and dislikes.

Hammad and Barhum would sometimes slip into the lecture halls of the Philosophy Department to listen, with their friend Alaa, to lectures by Dr. Yusuf Murad, Mustafa Swayf, Uthman Amin, and Ahmad Fouad al-Ahwani. There were more philosophy students than Arabic language students, so they were entitled to a lecture hall and microphone. Uthman Amin talked and joked well and made do with referring the students to his books. Dr. Ahmad al-Ahwani, on the other hand, was absorbed in his subject and shone in analyzing it in an unhurried manner and soft voice. He seemed nice to the point of naivety at times. A Moroccan friend related that he hadn't been able to finish his fourth-year research on time. He handed it in late and began making excuses about how he had been occupied with the problems of his country and family. Al-Ahwani looked at him and asked his name.

"Abd al-Qadir al-Shunqayti," the student replied.

"Are you from the mujahideen?" al-Ahwani asked.

The student nodded his head in assent. "Okay. I'll just give you twelve out of twenty," said the teacher.

On certain special occasions Cairo University would become a site of activity and interest beyond the sphere of lessons and exams. Hammad remembered in particular the day Gamal Abd al-Nasser visited the university in 1958 during the Science Festival and delivered a speech before the teachers and students in the Grand Hall. Hammad and his friends were seated on the second story and on their left, on a balcony extending over the lower hall, was a group of female students which included two leaders who belonged to the Baath Party at the time, a Syrian girl called Nihad Mustafa, and a Palestinian girl called Naila Abd al-Hadi. Before the speech they led a chorus of shouting, "One Arab nation!" which the rest of the students repeated enthusiastically and exuberantly. During Nasser's speech they interrupted him from time to time shouting their slogan, "Unity! Socialist freedom!" and the students would clamor after them for up to three minutes while Nasser smiled and waited. Union between Egypt and Syria was imminent and, now that the pressure of the secret police had been eased, the Baathists were energetic and active. The image stuck in Hammad's mind of this group of female students, led by Nihad and Naila, standing on the balcony of the second story and shouting slogans while Nasser watched and waited to be allowed to resume speaking. There was a sense of optimism in the air, after the Tripartite Aggression had failed and Nasser had emerged as a giant leader and statesman focused on implementing the nationalist program. The newspapers and radio filled people's eyes and ears and did not allow the opportunity to hear other views or read criticism of Nasser's regime. During the summer holiday, when he traveled to Morocco, Hammad read some of this criticism, but his attraction to Nasser's candor and courage soon dispelled his misgivings, suspended his critical abilities, and made him tend to disbelieve accounts of the severity with which the regime dealt with Egyptian communist activists, especially after 1959.

When Hammad recalled the four years he spent at university, he saw himself like a moth drawn to a bright, blinding lamp, hovering and rushing to pierce the perimeter of light, finding the passage of days and seasons too slow. His discoveries outside university kindled the dream that had beguiled him while in secondary school. Throughout university he wrote short stories and read them to his friends. When he heard about a competition organized by the Story Club, he submitted a story and was placed sixteenth, with encouragement to keep writing from members of the judging panel. It was as though university awakened his curiosity and made him see that the four-year journey was simply the beginning of another journey, which would not end except to begin again far away from certificates and success in exams. Perhaps what he experienced during these years were just illusions and specters of events, encounters, and learning, all of them blurred. It was as though they were recorded on the parchment but now, as he tried to visualize them, he was simply writing over that parchment, so that words and lines emerged before him that were different to what he grasped at the time. As he wrote he surrendered to the game of memory and its phantoms. It was like watching motions, signs, and words on a moving screen, which created the illusion of a continuity of scenes, connected in every measurement to the kingdom of nothingness.

Extensions

Hammad visited Cairo University again in December of 1971. He was living in Paris, preparing his thesis on the critical works of Muhammad Mandour, and needed some sources and to speak to Mandour's wife, the poet Malak Abd al-Aziz. When he entered the university library, he noticed signs of decay and neglect as he examined clippings and moved about the hoards of books and magazines. He visited the Arabic Language Department and inquired about his teachers, and paid his respects to those who were still there. The corridors and classrooms were bustling as usual with all kinds of people. He tried to visualize himself in this space that had so enchanted him as a student. Maybe something had changed deep inside him. Perhaps his experience at the Sorbonne had dampened his passion. Nevertheless, he thought that Cairo University deserved more attention in order to maintain its place in a fast-changing world. He felt a melancholy take hold of him during that visit. Nasser was dead and the Sadat era had begun dubiously, full of speeches and canny public statements. The anxiety was clear in his friends, who anticipated bad things and predicted that some of the positive accomplishments of Nasser would be dissolved. They would relate a joke that epitomized the mindset of 'the leader of believers.' The joke was that at the crossroads the driver would ask Sadat whether to go left or right. Sadat would ask the driver which way Nasser had gone. He would reply that he had turned left, so Sadat would tell him to signal left but turn right.

At the time Hammad remembered the small book Muhammad Mandour published four months after the 1952 Revolution entitled *Political Democracy*, in which he stressed the need for the return of democracy in order to safeguard a phase in which all powers would be accommodated, the struggle would be clear, and accountability would be possible in an atmosphere of intellectual pluralism and freedom of opinion. It was short but it was written with a force and zeal reminiscent of Mandour's articles around the time that the Council of Workers and Students was established in 1946, envisioning a future with pillars fixed on democratic foundations that balanced liberal thinking with the common rights of the citizen. But history seldom complied with what seemed logical and rational. It always had a greater logic and truth. For who would deny that Nasser, for over fifteen years, had convinced everyone that the revolution was constructed on the plane of reality and that he had almost every voice calling for the fight for freedom and socialist reform? There was little point in saying it was the wrong decision after the dust had cleared from the battlefield, because the crucial act was carried out amid the whirlpool, with all the risks of adventure and failure.

On that visit to Cairo, Hammad was absorbed in trying to understand the reasons why he chose the critical works of Mandour as the subject of his thesis. He had seen him once at an Arab Writers' Conference in Cairo in 1958, to which he and his friend Barhum had gone to pay respect to the late Abdallah Kanun, who was speaking for Morocco, and there became acquainted with the faces of eminent writers like Mikhail Nu'ayma, Mahmoud al-Masaadi, Suhayl Idris, Ahmad Abbas Salih, and Yusuf Idris. Hammad remembered Mandour interrupting to challenge al-Masaadi's talk, which was bold and countered prevailing opinion on the necessity of commitment in literature. Mandour walked as though dragging his feet, which, Hammad would learn later, was because his pituitary gland had been removed. His loud voice was convincing in its argument and shone in its criticisms. Hammad used to read the articles he published in *al-Sha'b* newspaper and in other magazines articulating the features of a more critical and committed literature, and he remembered relying on Mandour's books when preparing lectures after becoming a teacher at the College of Arts in Rabat. During this period, he had begun to consolidate his understanding of critical methods in France and to reconsider things he had read and studied. While living and studying in Paris he contemplated the possibility of re-examining contemporary Arabic criticism in light of his findings in critical and literary theory.

He gradually became convinced that investigating Mandour's book *New Method* could only proceed through analysis and criticism of available discourses. Mandour's case was important and representative, as he did not make do with affiliation to the university but occupied a place in the general field of literary criticism through his articles, studies, books, and polemics, and in the political realm through his membership of the Wafdist Left, participation in parliament, and openness to the younger generation. Yet Hammad, who reread Mandour's writings carefully and deliberately, sensed a notable contradiction: the French critical tools and skills on which Mandour relied were marked by a high degree of abridgment and premature interpretation, while his articles and comments met with approval and, even at a distance, touched on questions that were current in the field of modern Arabic literature. How could this be explained? Was the superficial use of concepts and technical terms that Hammad perceived the basis of the difference between modern French criticism, which participated in cultivating knowledge and questions, and Arabic criticism, which seemed unable to mount the new creativity and mobilize the stagnant field away from merely regurgitating loose and general interpretations?

After a year and a half of studying, analyzing, and making notes, Hammad felt that whenever he took a step forward he entered a maze, or that he was riding a blinkered, galloping horse. Were studies and articles enough to grasp the true essence of a writer? The biography of the critic or writer may not be fundamental to analysis, but would analyzing his discourse not bring you closer to his thought and the influence he had on people? Although at the outset Hammad had decided not to concern himself with Mandour's biography and to deal with his writings as though they were independent of the author's personal life, he became anxious about transforming a person of flesh and blood and emotion into a subject to be studied from a certain distance and on the basis of concepts and technical terms whose theoretical applicability blossomed in a different cultural context. He hastened to review his notes, attempting to find a way to subjugate, correlate, and give concepts new life in a socio-intellectual context teeming with the life and events of Egypt between 1936 and 1960. The project was exciting but surrounded by dangerous pitfalls. During this time, Hammad decided to visit Cairo to gather more material and speak to people close to Mandour, for although he had decided against the critic's biography as an approach, question marks kept raising their heads to remind him that what he was studying was written in specific circumstances, that affected the critic, his tensions, and responses, and that redressing 'the method' did not mean replacing the person with the subject and sympathetic analysis with cold dissection.

When Hammad arrived in Cairo in mid-December 1971, a slight chill was spreading in the early evening and the passing clouds announced late rain. He met his friends and enjoyed staying up into the night with them. He visited Sayyida Malak Abd al-Aziz in the quarter of al-Manyal and questioned her about Mandour's readings, work pattern, pursuit of literature and drama, and relations with academic and cultural institutions. She answered him with utmost kindness and characteristic politeness. As he wandered through the Cairo streets, he was pursued by the image of Mandour with his beret on his head, walking slowly and talking easily and powerfully on the platform at the Arab Writers' Conference in 1958. He smiled wryly at the hypotheses and analyses he had applied in order to interpret, over more than twenty years, the critic's many writings. He immersed himself in thought each day, making notes and adjusting his conclusions in order to relieve the weight he had begun to collapse under as a result of this 'return' of Mandour, a man connected to a particular space and the concerns of his people. He was surprised when New Year's Day came and he didn't have any plans. He hesitated: should he go out for the evening or carry on with his papers? He decided to go out and observe people in the streets and have a drink to take him away from questions of criticism and the critic. He dressed in trousers and a leather jacket and put a brown cap he had brought with him from Paris on his head. The streets of Cairo that evening were busy and the clamor he loved took him back to the old days. He walked along, studying faces and picking up fragments of conversation and laughter. He felt lonely and faced with questions he did not have the power to answer. He decided to come out of his seclusion and approach two young girls, one of whom had black smiling eyes and a tanned face, rendering her mesamsema—delicate featured—as Egyptians say. When he was alongside them he began talking in French. They were surprised and didn't understand what he was saying so walked on. He followed them, uttering words in French from time to time and gesturing with his hands. They would pause for a minute then resume walking, commenting, and laughing about the behavior of the French stranger. He played his role assiduously until the mesamsema girl turned to him and said in a loud voice, "For God's sake, go to the Domiaty and eat fuul. It's better than hassling girls." He could not restrain his laughter and spun around quickly, his chuckles attracting the attention of passersby. Twenty years had passed since that little episode, but he still remembered the mesamsema girl's face and the charm that exposed him as a bad actor.

Another time he recalled the atmosphere of Cairo University without visiting it. This was in Beirut in the mid-1970s when he came across Naila Abd al-Hadi, one of the two leaders who interrupted Nasser during his speech in the Grand Hall. He introduced himself and told her that he was at the university on that memorable day. She smiled and said sadly, "Unrepeatable days . . . ." She introduced her husband as a businessman and when Hammad asked a friend about him, he said he became rich because he knew how to profit from regimes of "unity and socialism," which needed weapons and electronic means of oppression on the pretext of preparing for the liberation of Palestine. The man had taken advantage of his wife's reputation and party connections in the days of the student struggle. Naila spoke neutrally and in a language that preserved national honor but didn't actually say anything, while her husband remained silent or nodded his head in agreement. Hammad spent a long time considering the gift that enabled a person to speak without saying anything. Florid statements and arguments that said nothing, which you listened to without gaining anything. It wasn't easy. Indeed, it was harder than expressing deep meanings and clear opinions. She was entitled to change, Hammad thought to himself. It would not erase from his memory those glittering moments at Cairo University with the group of female students shouting wonderful slogans while Nasser gazed at them, smiling. It was fortunate that when people regressed from his idealized dreams Hammad could not erase from his memory the moments that encapsulated them.

But oversentimentality and deification can harm those we love. Hammad remembered this as he read, on the occasion of a recent commemoration of the revolution of July 23, a statement by someone who worked with Nasser and was close to him. The former politician said eloquently, "If Nasser came back he would spit on us and return to his grave!" What could one conclude from these words other than that their owner needed to spit in order to feel that he existed? The leader had died with his merits and faults and had left the way open for each person to assume responsibility, but this man still insisted that Nasser continue to rule from beyond the grave with an authority that was condescending and contemptuous toward the citizen who erred. A stream of expressions and coined questions repeated by newspapers and magazines on special occasions and a pack of familiar answers. What would the messiah say if he returned from the grave? What about Muhammad Ali? Samia Gamal? Ismail Yasin? Hammad ironically surmised that if the latter did return he would say to the former politician, "Get lost! Go eat fuul—yes you—at the Domiaty."

Umm Fathiya

Like Umm Fathiya: "A black bride adorned with pearl necklaces."

No one could remember how they first got to know her or agreed with her that she would take care of the housekeeping at the flat they rented in 1957 in Zamalek. The flat was between the building's entrance and the basement; but then Zamalek was all alleys. With the regular arrival of the grant, it was inevitable that the three of them—Barhum, Alaa, and Hammad—would be left to themselves to face the phase of university and the trappings of bachelorhood, and to discover some of life's pleasures after a year of primitive living and poverty at the North African Lodge.

Umm Fathiya was in her forties. Her black skin was smooth and her long face was distinguished by small eyes whose pupils rarely stayed still and a smile that seemed to issue straight from her eyes. Her manner was natural and she spoke sweetly with the slight stutter that was common in Egyptianized Nubians. When she talked about her origins she wasn't clear about where she came from—Sudan or Nubia. She always wore a black gallabiya and a veil of the same color; bright colors were only seen when she took it off. She was quite small but her dynamism meant she filled the room.

Hammad was responsible for the food budget, therefore his relationship with Umm Fathiya was not free from wrangling, especially in times of difficulty, when money was scarce and the arrival of the grant was delayed. Each morning negotiations got going to reach an agreement over the contents of lunch and what would be left over for supper. On days of poverty they usually resorted to white beans and rice, which was dirt cheap, and tomato salad. Whenever Hammad gave Umm Fathiya ten piasters she would respond with the same phrase, which became proverbial, "Today I'm going to make something just right for you," and it was tacitly understood that the food that day would consist of a solid meal of rice and beans or potatoes or lentils. On days of relative abundance Umm Fathiya was versatile and conjured up what she had learned and perfected while work-ing for Italian, French, and German employers: baked macaroni, potato gratin, purée, beefsteak with creamed mushrooms. . . . She was at her happiest and would scrounge a cigarette from Alaa Bey and enjoy herself as she laid the table and talked about the banquets and feasts she prepared single-handedly once upon a time. The three knights would sometimes get her to confess how she would drink beer and wine when her foreign employers persuaded her to. They would set aside a place for her to sit so that they could enjoy her stories while she sipped glasses of cold Stella. She would sit cross-legged on the floor and ask for a ciga-rette then grab the glass and raise it to the health of her Moroccan boys, "You're wonderful. God is great. I'm happy with you. You study hard and like having fun. Though sometimes you have too much. I see the signs when I come in the morning. Right Ustaz Barhum?" (Laughter.)

By the third glass, Umm Fathiya's expression would be merry and symptoms of light intoxication would show in her smile. She would speak more freely, especially when they asked her views on politics and Nasser: "What do you say, boys? You can laugh but I tell you, perhaps we'll get communism. Isn't communism the system that allows us to eat, have a house, and be treated in hospital for free? It's better than what we've got. We work so much but don't live well. So many people live wretchedly, poor them."

Laughter and enthusiastic remarks: "Bravo Umm Fathiya! You're a great political thinker. Where did you get this talk from?"

Umm Fathiya would giggle and lean on her right hand to hoist herself up.

"You're having a good time. You want to get me drunk. It's seven o'clock. Umm Hamdi will have sent her son to wait for me at the bus stop," she would say.

Thus Umm Fathiya's treasures were unveiled through her strong yet compliant personality and through her attitudes and experiences. Barhum, Alaa, and Hammad circulated some of her ideas and eccentricities among friends and she gained a reputation among the Moroccan students, especially those who visited the flat to meet her and enjoy her cooking. One day a group of friends were round and Umm Fathiya was in her element telling stories and answering questions. Perhaps the melody of Stella flowing in her veins let her drift off into make-believe and encouraged her to embellish her tales. One of them said to her, "Umm Fathiya, you're in your element, almost completely drunk. You should be in a film. We need to find her a director to appreciate her talents, right guys?"

"He said the movies . . . . All I know is that when I was only fifteen I acted in a film with Umm Kulthum, the film where she sings "Lovers, They Ask Me," you know?"

Laughter and disbelief. Umm Fathiya added, "By Hamdi's life, it's true. Go and ask Umm Kulthum. She'll tell you!"

When Hammad asked her about her roots, whether she was from Sudan or Nubia, and how she came to settle in Cairo, she would reply vaguely that she migrated with her father from Wadi Halfa when she was small. ("Have you heard of it? It's near Abu Simbel.") Her father was looking for work and his relatives in Cairo helped him out. He worked as a doorman until he died. She went to school for a short while then began working in houses, helping her mother: "Life depends on luck and on what kind of luck you have. After that my mother married me to an officer who was a horseman in the cavalry. He gave me my daughter Fathiya but died five years later. I brought Fathiya up and taught her, then she married a koshari-seller from Sayyida Zaynab. . . . That's the story. We're alive, thank God. We have enough."

In 1959, in their third year at university, they moved to a flat in Doqqi not far from the university. They lived in a two-story building, renting the first floor from Sitt Zaynat, who lived with her son and two daughters, also on the first floor. Sitt Zaynat was a thick-set woman who had a strong personality and was a good storyteller. Umm Fathiya was impressed by the flat and preferred it to the basement in Zamalek. When Eid al-Adha drew near, the three knights, together with two of their friends, decided to buy a ram to slaughter so that they could enjoy its tender meat and celebrate Eid in the Moroccan manner. Umm Fathiya's eyes widened and she smiled in wonder at the happy news. She quickly informed them that she and her half-brother, Radwan, would take responsibility for buying the ram at a price that would please them. Hammad suggested that he accompany her to the souq but she answered decisively, "Don't trouble yourself. My brother Radwan is a butcher. It's his job. Just tell me if you want it slaughtered or if you'd like to slaughter it here?"

"Of course we want to slaughter it here, Umm Fathiya, so the neighbors know that we're making an Eid sacrifice. . . . See?"

It was a memorable day. Lots of noise and excitement. Master Radwan in his vest, peasant trousers, and cotton skullcap, with his knives and deep bronchial expressions, and the Moroccan students in shorts, fetching buckets of water and helping turn the ram to face the direction of Mecca. It was hung and skinned and the liver and fat were prepared so they could be rolled for the traditional breakfast on the morning of Eid in Morocco. Tapes of Andalusian music played and cups of mint tea were passed round. Umm Fathiya was as happy as could be and looked proud in front of her half-brother, Master Radwan. They decided to finish the ram that day. They cooked lunch then dinner and what remained was distributed between Umm Fathiya and Master Radwan, with a taste for Sitt Zaynat and her family. The next day Hammad informed Umm Fathiya that they were entering a week of asceticism during which they would remember white beans, rice, potatoes, and lentils!

In June 1960, the results of the College of Arts were announced. The three friends had passed and preparations to return to Morocco began. They sensed the emptiness and longing that leaving Umm Fathiya would leave in their hearts: her colluding smile, conversation, comments, little skirmishes, and the friendship that words could not describe. They could not leave without visiting her at her home behind Abdin Square, where she lived with her married daughter in a two-room basement. They found her presiding over a small room, surrounded by her female neighbors from the basement, her daughter Fathiya and her husband, and their son Hamdi, who was nine and seemed shy despite the signs of mischief in his intelligent eyes. "Welcome, please come in. The quarter celebrates. These are my boys but alas they're going home and leaving me." "You should go with them," said a neighbor. "That's what we said but she doesn't want to. She says she needs to raise Hamdi," said Hammad. She laughed. "No, I told them I would go on the condition that they live together in Morocco too, even when they get married. Then I'll live with them forever."

Umm Fathiya was proud of the visit and of her boys, who had obtained their degrees and would return to their country to take up important posts. She tirelessly related memories of the happy days that she had spent with them over three years: "Good kids, really. They get on like brothers and their house is always full of friends, boys and girls, right Ustaz Hammad? They're also moody. And the Egyptian girls, so sweet! But we only have one life, and is anybody taking anything from it anyway?" She turned to Hamdi. "Listen Hamdi. You must study hard like them so you can go to university and graduate and we'll be proud of you. Right? Please advise him. He just plays with a ball all day. . . ."

The visit drew on and they wanted to say goodbye but Umm Fathiya entreated them to stay for a meal of koshari, specially prepared by her daughter's husband. "You'll eat your fingers afterward," she said. They formed a circle around the low round table and the talk and laughter was nonstop. Hammad leaned over to Umm Fathiya and whispered, "Shall we go and get you a bottle of Stella?" She hushed him, laughing, and whispered, "No, dear! Do you want to expose me in front of the neighbors? Leave it until tomorrow when I come and see you off."

When Hammad returned to Cairo in 1964 for a few weeks he was eager to visit Umm Fathiya. She could hardly believe it and began scolding him, "Is this acceptable, Hammad? Only one letter in all these years. . . . Didn't we know each other well? Living together is not taken lightly except by the illegitimate." Hammad kissed her forehead and made excuses about work and looking for somewhere to settle and assured her that she was always in his mind and heart. He gave her a Moroccan kaftan of brocade and lace and urged her to put it on. Then he put a yellow belt made from Sicilian thread around her waist, so that she looked "beautiful and radiant like a bourgeois Moroccan woman." He laughed and said to her, "Don't worry. We'll take a photo and look for a groom for you!"

Like a snake, days curl up and wrap people in their vortex leaving nothing behind except new memories. Thoughts like these seduced Hammad in 1972 when he visited Cairo after years filled with work, travel, and adventures. He was coming from Paris, where he was living and preparing his doctoral thesis. As he looked down at the houses and buildings by the Cairo train station, the image of Umm Fathiya popped into his head. Goodness! He hadn't seen her for eight years. He would visit her first thing tomorrow he thought, hoping that she was still alive.

He was shocked to find that the basement she lived in had disappeared and a tall building had been erected in its place. He circled the quarter a few times and asked after Umm Fathiya and her family. With difficulty he located the doorman of the building next door, who told him that they had left three years ago. He had heard them talking about Afrah al-Angal Alley, behind Muhammad Ali Street, where they had found a room on a roof. Hammad was determined to find Umm Fathiya so he asked the way to the alley and began questioning residents house by house, offering descriptions, but no one knew Umm Fathiya and the inhabitants of Afrah al-Angal had not grown in ten years! "Really?" "Yes. It's true," said a cobbler crouching in a small shop at one end of the alley. "I know everyone here without exception. It's my job. Some people have died but no one new has come, no."

Hammad spent three days searching for Umm Fathiya in the popular quarters without finding any trace of her. He was sure that what he was doing was completely useless in the vast and crowded city of Cairo without anything to go on. But he couldn't accept that Umm Fathiya was lost to him, for he was used to the idea that she would be around forever, that he could meet her whenever he visited or whenever he felt a yearning for her. In the last few years he had read about Nubia, visited exhibitions of Nubian statues and inscriptions, and watched documentaries about the area full of antiquities and Nile rapids. He pictured Umm Fathiya and surrendered to his imagination, pretending that she had not left all that beauty to live in a poor city quarter, neglected and separated from her birthplace. He was determined that this time he would talk to her about Ramesses II, who built underground temples and decorated tombs and caverns with inscriptions etched into the rocks. He intended to ask her to return to Nubia, or rather he wanted to suggest that he go with her to reclaim her roots, breathe the pure air of the oases and bathe in the clear waters of the Nile. Here no one knew her, and her family lived in wretchedness and poverty, while there her pores would open to the breezes, sun's rays, and songs. Across the plains of Wadi al-Subu, Wadi Halfa, and Abu Simbel, she could walk proudly with her suntanned skin and small body, which traced back to the descendents of Mandulis, the ancient god of Nubia. There she could wander about the thickets, the caves of Philae, and the sacred island of Isis, and realize her dream of a happy life that would compensate her hard work and didn't enslave the weak. Umm Fathiya, in his opinion, with her acumen, goodness, and love of life, deserved to be a princess in the pagan kingdom of Nubia, which upheld the freedom of living beings. Plants, trees, animals, people, and gods filled this space that was deeply rooted in ancient times and watched over the fate of God's creatures. Hammad remembered the caption beneath an ancient painting depicting the upper half of a legend-ary princess with a long neck, open mouth, and head raised to the sky: "The cry that this creature wants to hear, in vain, is a reverberating Hallelujah lost amid the everlasting silence."

At the end of that visit to Cairo, Hammad felt that he had lost something valuable: something that was a part of his accumulated self, in which he would seek refuge to combat triviality, turbidity, and feelings of extinction. In times that followed he tried again to look for Umm Fathiya but without success. Then he became fond of this unexpected ending. Perhaps it was better, he said to himself. Umm Fathiya was preserved in his memory bursting with vitality and splendor. Her words dwelled inside me and she was herself—the woman from an ancient soil and from the lowlands of Cairo, surrounded by a halo of talk, smiles, and laughter, thus simultaneously immersed in and separated from her surroundings. The fact that she worked for them was not all that brought him and his friends together with Umm Fathiya. What did you call the kind of relationship that mutated into magnetic moments, which barely twinkled in your memory before you became speechless with joy and happiness and something words could not describe? A relationship that had a date and time but soon transcended them and became an essential part of one's deepest self. Hammad accepted this ending because it meant that Umm Fathiya stayed in his memory, safe from old age and released from death. He could not imagine her as an old lady or lying in the hollow of a grave. She would always be as he knew her: sprightly, smiling, quick-witted, living in the heart of Cairo or slipping off to Wadi al-Subu to bathe in the sacred waters of the Nile and be enriched by the splendor of Isis.

Ambiguous
Relationships

WITH HER GENTLE MELANCHOLY smile and well-proportioned brown body, Fawziya had illuminated new aspects of body language and tenderness for Hammad and opened the gates wide before his fantasies. She was a fitting 'introduction' for the country of rosy, romantic films that tickled his imagination as a small boy in Fez. He couldn't remember how the relationship with Fawziya ended, but tended to attribute it to him becoming immersed in the throng of ambiguous relationships that began with the arrival of the grant, renting a flat, and his gravitation to the things Cairo had to offer young men.

During the first year of university, Hammad tried to get a feel for the fair sex through the female students, but it became clear that it was a tedious task and that affection which promised future marriage was the only route into a relationship. This was a general rule and appeared natural and comforting for members of the middle or lower classes, who worked hard to establish themselves and believed in a future based on relatively moderate and liberal values. But Hammad was not looking for a relationship whose ceiling was determined from the outset by marriage. He didn't even know what his circumstances would be after he graduated and returned home, especially as his mother and three brothers were waiting for someone to provide for them. Thus his relationship with the female students turned into one of friendship and chatter, and he began looking for romance outside the university. It was Abduh who guided his steps on this path. Abduh returned from Morocco at the end of 1956 with a large sum of money, given to him by his mother, who used to spoil him and was very proud that her son was studying in Egypt. Abduh was bold and foolhardy and fond of the world of seduction, his talents in this area revealed while still at secondary school in Rabat. When he returned with full pockets he felt sorry for Hammad and the rest of the group, who were burying themselves in papers and books instead of discovering the other side of Cairo, the fun side, which was captivating with its liberal women, magical dancers, and spellbinding singers. To prove the truth of his claims, he invited his friends, Hammad and Barhum, to enjoy something that he had begun to enjoy three or four times a week. It was Hammad's first time in a cabaret with dancers. Abduh ordered a bottle of champagne, crossed his legs, lit a cigarette, and began encouraging the dancer and uttering loud expressions of delight. Hammad was amazed and gripped by the dancer as she twisted and smiled. Her body's powers could stir even the ifreets among the jinn. Abduh was enraptured as he sipped his champagne and urged his friends to drink and to wait for the surprise that would come when the dancer "Susu" ascended the stage in a little while. There were some Gulf Arabs at the cabaret too, who were dressed in elaborate white robes and ornate headbands and who were enjoying much attention from the waiter and cabaret-owner. Abduh imitated them in distributing tips and renewing orders for drinks. When Susu appeared in full dancing regalia, revealing her magical qualities and concealing as little as possible, Abduh jumped up clapping and cheering, as did the Gulf Arabs and some old-time Egyptians. With his small frame and handsome young face, Abduh was like a pistachio nut in a date thicket. Nevertheless, Susu singled him out with a smiling look, which alerted Hammad and Barhum's curiosity. When things got really hot and the dancer's body language, drumbeat, and fans' enthusiasm were blazing, Susu began to descend the stairs toward the men sitting at single tables at the front of the room. Her patrons stood up and placed large banknotes between her breasts. Abduh rose lightly and gracefully, took hold of the dancer's fingers and summoned her to step up onto the table, placing a chair at her feet and notes in her cleavage. She smiled as she stepped onto the table and danced over the heads of Abduh and his two stunned friends. Before long the Gulf Arabs summoned her to honor their tables, while Abduh savored the dancer's response to him and his superiority over his neighbors, who copied him.

Thus Abduh opened the way for some of his friends to unexplored parts of Cairo. But Hammad and Barhum's budget was not as generous as the one that their friend obtained and managed so, together with Alaa, they satisfied themselves with weekly get-togethers with three beautiful, chic girls, who had some education and were charming company but demanded a fee for their gratifying visits. Each girl attached herself to one of them, lending the relationships, whose basis was clear, a certain personal quality. Meetings with Nawal, Ilham, and Hikmat began to take place regularly on Thursday afternoons and followed a ritual of private time in the bedroom and sitting communally in the living room, flirting, joking, and drinking refreshing drinks. Sometimes the meeting ended with dinner or an invitation to a café on the banks of the Nile. Yet even when a relationship is this transparent, the close association produces seeds of ambiguity and tender intimacy.

Hammad sometimes forgot the nature of his relationship with Nawal and would get carried away with sentimental expressions, which were not reciprocated on the other side except for the duration of the Thursday visit, after which she would withdraw into her secrets and private life. The three knights were all confused about why the three women got involved in such relationships in spite of their social position and education, but gradually aspects of their background came to light through the chatter and questions, and their understanding of their difficult financial circumstances became clearer. Each of them had a story of unrequited love or a knight who had deceived her, but the stories all flowed into one: people like them had multiple relationships in order to fulfill their need for clothes, finery, spending money, and indeed to help their families. However, they still preserved the hope of marriage if time should be so generous as to provide a "fine groom" seeking a housewife who observed principles according to outward gauges. What about the issue of virginity, the three knights asked. The girls laughed loudly, astonished by the repressed Moroccan students who hadn't heard about the simple operations that restored virginity to virgins. "Really?" "Absolutely!" And the proof was that Barhum's girlfriend, Hikmat, was getting married next month and would be having the operation two days before the wedding night, and they must wish her good fortune and happiness and help her cover the operation's costs. Thus Hammad and his two friends realized that they were living in "an era of patching up tears," which permitted strangers and those unable to afford an engagement ring and bear the expenditure of a wedding to steal some pleasure and quench their thirst in secret, safe from calamity while outwardly upholding principles. Years later, at the beginning of the 1980s, Hammad would discover that some

Moroccan girls from the lower and middle classes were also playing a part in a phase of "patching up tears" in order not to clash with their families when the opportunity to marry came along. As he contemplated the phenomenon he said to himself: what the girls in Egypt were doing in the fifties, Moroccan girls are doing in the eighties. Aspects of Egyptian society's past had become part of Moroccan society's future. Surely there were differences but he couldn't see them.

The day approached for Hikmat's farewell to devote herself to "patching up the tear" and receiving her groom. Barhum was restless, for the close association that had been going on for over a year had left its mark. But this was the way of the world and he must say goodbye with more grace than he received and hearten her to a happy, stable life. Ilham interrupted the atmosphere of laughter and drinking with a sad and disconcerting monologue which cut short the flow of farewell and encouragement. "I often ask myself: where's the justice, sisters? Why am I, Ilham Abd al-Sami Ragab, respected employee at the ministry of endowments, forced to sell my body? No offense Alaa. I like you and have a good time with you, but the relationship is still tied to material profit for me. It has no other horizon. It's not the life I wanted but what can I do?" Alaa had told Hammad about his pleasurable times with Ilham, who had a pretty round face and tender-skinned body, and Hammad was happy with the dark-skinned Nawal and her Cairene coquettishness and large breasts, even though she told him openly that she had other lovers. The moment of Hikmat's farewell drew near and Barhum delivered a sensitive, romantic speech, as though addressing her in the days when she was still a virgin. Her own reply was brief, "Only God knows what's in our hearts. We'll leave our friendship to time. Who knows if we'll meet again one day." It was a bit of melodrama worthy of one of Hasan Imam's films, but Hammad still felt that they were engulfed by a breeze of friendship which had an aroma of beautiful ambiguity despite the clear facts of the situation.

Hammad recalled other fleeting relationships, some of them full of fun, others far removed from that ambiguous transparency. The source of variation was linked to the change in living quarters between Doqqi, al-Masaha, and Zamalek (in a respectable basement, nonetheless). He became acquainted with a nurse who worked in a clinic in Helwan, who had delicate features and a sweet smile though was shy and reticent to a degree that did not match her occupation. She refused to visit him at the flat and limited their meetings to Nile casinos and holding hands. One day he decided to visit her at the clinic and convince her to accompany him home. They sat on the balcony of the clinic café and she was delighted by his visit, but uneasy with the glances of her male and female colleagues. They talked for a while and he tried to kiss her but she broke free. Her cheeks turned red and she asked him not to cause her problems. She said it was best that the relationship went no further.

Another time he became acquainted with a young girl who was 'lost,' having come to Cairo looking for work but not found the relatives she was hoping to live with. She stayed with Hammad in the flat for several days but was determined to preserve her virginity. She would disappear for a week or more then return, and it was understood by his two friends that the relationship was special. They talked a lot and he asked her about her life and her confrontation with society. She had a strong personality and was generous in her affections, but she kept her secrets buried, conscious of where the boundaries lay.

Besides these special relationships there were others that opened on to surprises and laughter. Hammad remembered that they rented a flat in al-Masaha owned by William Bey, whom Barhum had met at some occasion. William Bey—as Barhum called him—was an accountant for a building contractor's company. He was married with children and took care to look elegant and comb and gel his hair. After a while, he started visiting them in the flat and asking them about college, the female students, and their adventures in Cairo. He was in his forties but seemed full of youth, vitality, and masculinity. He suggested to Barhum that they all spend an evening at the flat and that he invite along a liberal friend of his who liked meeting Arab students. Alaa had an appointment that evening so the gathering was confined to Hammad, Barhum, William Bey, and Muna. It became clear as they drank and the formality lifted that the visitor did not want to waste the evening talking and listening to William Bey flirting. When she had spent time alone with the two friends it was William Bey's turn, and he was waiting on tenterhooks. He tried to hurry her in the intermission but she rebuffed him and began humiliating him: "Enough William. I'm tired today. Next time." He kept on begging and flirted doubly hard but she repelled him. Indeed she slapped his cheek when he offered her his face: "Slap me if you like but please don't deny me. I want to sleep with you."

Barhum and Hammad thought the issue was straightforward and that it was easy enough for the married William Bey to respect Muna's wishes. But he persisted in humiliating himself and she continued to insult and deny him. The atmosphere became tense and they were forced to intervene and convince him to postpone for another day. When he was convinced his wish was impossible his smile soon returned. He arranged his clothes and tie and offered to give Muna a lift home in his car. Before he left he whispered in Barhum's ear that he needed the keys to the apartment the next day because he was bringing another friend. Hammad and Barhum laughed a lot as they recalled the scene of Muna with William Bey kneeling at her feet surrendering to flirtatious drivel and receiving her blows. They later learned that William Bey had an obsession for daily denigration. His wife did not respond to his abundant appetites so he found a solution this way, sometimes suffering disgrace and humiliation.

Hammad remembered the story of their Moroccan friend Darnkali, who used to spend his grant on books and eating and drinking in restaurants then go round the houses of friends to borrow from them while he waited for the next installment. It became a habit and they would prepare their excuses or only lend him a small sum, as they knew from past experience that the debt would not be repaid. One time he visited them early in the afternoon and found two girls passing by to say hello and see how they were. Hammad and his friends did not pay him much attention and carried on chatting and laughing. Darnkali immersed himself in the gathering, lending it his cheer and glamour. One of the girls thought she could tempt him so said that she wanted one of them to write a letter to her friend in Ismailiya. He saw a good opportunity and volunteered. He sat down beside her and the remarks didn't stop. "Come on, let's go to the room," she said. "They won't leave us alone." After a little Darnkali left, wearing only underwear and gesturing to his friends to lend him three pounds so he could write the letter. It was an amusing and awkward situation, and Hammad was forced to lend him some of the food budget. As usual Darnkali said, "What's money? The grant will arrive tomorrow and I'll pay you back in full!"

When the exams were approaching the three knights announced a state of emergency with regard to receiving friends and visitors and devoted themselves to revising lectures and memorizing what was required. Hammad remembered that he was with Barhum in the apartment one afternoon, absorbed in revision with the help of cups of tea and coffee. It was not particularly pleasant, especially when it came to philology and Hebrew, but they were eager to get through the exams. They heard the doorbell and Barhum went to open the door. He returned with a plump girl, her hair arranged as though she had come straight from the hairdresser, wearing a dark blue suit. She looked grave and was carrying a small bag in her hand. Hammad watched Barhum as he greeted her. "Your sister Anhar," she said. "I'm selling fine perfumes at cheap prices." Barhum's feigned innocent smile signaled that the perfumes were just a cover and there was no harm in interrupting the boredom of study to greet a new face. They examined the perfumes and found them to be ordinary so began talking to her about her adventures knocking on houses, especially those inhabited by bachelors. She answered cleverly and her intimations encouraged them to keep going toward what they guessed was behind the perfume game. After some time in the bedroom, they were sat drinking tea in the living room, talking and laughing, with Anhar wearing one of their dressing gowns, when Alaa suddenly opened the door of the flat and came in with a Lebanese friend of his, Fayza, who, with her amiableness, pretty face, and slender build, resembled a 'fayrouza'—a turquoise stone that eyes never tire of gazing at. Fayza was cultured, enthusiastic about Arabism, and loved music and art. Alaa held her in high esteem and harbored special feelings for her. To get back to the matter: Alaa (who knew that such meetings were not permitted at the time) opened the door to find his two friends sitting in their pajamas with a girl in a dressing gown in between them. In a moment of confusion Barhum was inspired to introduce Anhar as a journalist from the newspaper *al-Akhbar* who had come to interview them about student life and exams. But when she stood up to greet Alaa and Fayza the dressing gown fell open revealing the contours of her naked body! Alaa and his friend withdrew to his bedroom and Hammad and Barhum were embarrassed, for they thought highly of Fayza and shared mutual interests. They quickly saw off the perfume-seller and awaited their friend's anger and criticism from Fayza, who always condemned fleeting relationships.

During the year in Zamalek living in a basement flat next to some Asian diplomats, Hammad noticed that a beautiful woman would visit the neighbors at an appointed time each week. Her face resembled that of the actress Magda, with her sad features, and her body exuded the sensuality and seductiveness of Hind Rostom. After some persuasion she agreed to confer a weekly visit on the students' flat for a specified price. She seemed to harbor some sorrow or trauma or a secret, and her beauty did not match her sparse conversation, which was confined to a few words uttered quietly in a disjointed voice. She said that she was married and was forced to make visits of this nature. She refused to drink and did not bring much joy to the room. One day, early in the afternoon, a Moroccan friend came to visit, who was distinguished in his studies, shy and introverted. The beautiful wife was preparing to leave but introductions were made before she departed. A few days later the friend contacted Hammad and brought him round to talking about the visitor he had seen at the flat, and surprised him by asking him to arrange an appointment with her and to give her his address. He thought for a moment then added that he was living alone and his shyness prevented him from forming relationships, but he was attracted to the woman so had ventured to ask him to help arrange a date, if the woman had no ojections. Hammad thought highly of his friend and found it strange that he lived in solitude after a failed romance in Rabat. His introversion stifled his intellectual energy and immersed him in a heavy depression. So the appointment was arranged and the encounter between the timid friend and quiet beauty took place. When Hammad met up with his friend, he asked him how it went. He answered, "She's a beautiful woman. Too bad she is so unresponsive. It was like she wasn't there." Hammad was silent and pondered the reaction of his friend, whose own physique was not remarkable and who knew that the woman was forced into such meetings but in spite of this insisted that she be responsive. Perhaps he did not want a fleeting encounter but therapy for his solitude, which was something else. Nothing scrapes the skin like nails.

◎

Relaxing in the darkness and listening to music, or trying to sleep on a sleepless night, Hammad often recalled the paths of his sexual appetite and relationships with women from childhood to the beginning of adulthood. He recalled girls who indulged themselves and others who wore halos of timidity and purity. He remembered some of the details: the fear and stammering in the beginning, the persistent effort, and his body's excitement when he sensed that he was not alone in his journey. He wasn't trying to attach more significance to these ambiguous relationships than they merited or to vindicate them, but they had a pleasing aroma. Later he would read a remark by Sartre that caught his attention: "Even in a purely physical relationship a deep love can exist." It seemed to Hammad, beyond explanations and justifications, that these relationships were also a search, an inquisitiveness, a pursuit of fantasies etched between his pores and in the folds of his imagination since early childhood through images, stories, faces, and dreams. But lust was even more than that. It was not simply a response to what the world offered and the body pulsed with. It was, in Hammad's opinion, a longing to make sacrifices and to give, to understand the other person and fathom their desires, and to create relationships that transcended what seemed matter-of-fact and monotonous and smothered dreams. Lust seemed to him the prime engine, but who could guarantee that it would not be at the other's expense and run counter to their carnal desire? As long as he couldn't sleep the anxious questions kept coming. Hammad felt that lust, by good fortune, was never completely fulfilled. The course toward it always revealed it to be a mirage or flawed.

We keep striving for the 'perfect' realization of lust under the auspices of a love that cannot last: it seemed to Hammad that, in the time that followed, he experienced moments of that realization in France and Morocco, when he experienced love that ignited both body and soul. But even in those moments the ambiguity did not completely vanish. It was different to what he experienced in his ambiguous relationships, because love and sex, in competing for fulfillment, cannot escape the starkness of death, a tragic starkness but one that still has its appeal, so it seemed to Hammad.

Extensions

Hammad guessed that there were other modes of life and relationships in Cairo, different to the image woven by an ideological discourse that constantly searched for social embodiments that would never be fully realized. Yesterday's society, with its classes, rituals, and hidden secrets, had not disappeared. This was only natural.

A Moroccan friend who had lived in Cairo for a long time told him that by chance he became acquainted with a bourgeois lady who came from a background of wealth and luxury. She trusted him because he wasn't Egyptian and because he spoke French, which she liked, and because there was a sternness to his good looks. The relationship progressed and she told him frankly that for her pleasure was not self-contained but bound up with fantasies and surges that dwell in the body. "Of course," said the friend so as not to appear ignorant and added that he had read Freud's remarks on the subject. She smiled, reassured, "Excellent. I was afraid you wouldn't understand. Now I can enjoy our relationship." "Yeah, yeah," replied the friend. She shook the clothes from her tender, marble body and her eyes became a summons and longing cry. But she hastened to say, "Slowly. I want to be abused first. Mmm, your darling wants you to abuse and beat her as though she's offended you." Hammad's friend thought it over and said to himself that he was in a situation that clearly bordered on masochism. He gave her a hard slap. She sighed deeply and whispered, "God, you're so lovely." He flung himself on her compact arm and bit it while she demanded more. "You whore," he said. "Yes. What else?" "Prostitute." "Mmm, what else?" "Shameless." She turned onto her back. "Shameless of what? Of this? I love it. What do you call it in Morocco, isn't there another name for it? Ah, that's a better one. . . ."

Hammad's friend found himself, his body, and his lust in an unprecedented situation. The fact that he enjoyed it was confusing, unlike anything he had experienced before.

On a visit to Cairo in 1989, Hammad was staying at the apartment of a friend. One evening he was reading some newspapers, magazines, and books he had bought. Around eleven o'clock the telephone rang. "Allo? Can I talk to Muna?" said a coquettish female voice. "Muna is not here. I'm her cousin." "Really? She never told me she had a cousin with a voice as sweet as yours."

The conversation continued for almost half an hour. The girl spoke boldly and spontaneously about different subjects. She told Hammad that she was a pupil in secondary school but was fed up and wanted to live and experience sex, even though she was not yet fifteen. He tried to calm her down but she responded defiantly, "What future and what studies, sheikh? You sound foreign. I want to live. Tell you what. Let's meet now and find a boat on the Nile." Hammad dodged as she besieged him with suggestions and embarrassing questions about his body, what he was wearing, and where his hand was while he was talking to her. With difficulty he convinced her to postpone their chat to the next day. When the conversation was over he suddenly felt old, as though the secret part of Cairo that he had known in the age of "patching up tears" had moved into a new phase of "post-tear."

Hammad sometimes felt he went too far and got carried away with a single vision, led by his selective memory. Why didn't he remember things that caught his attention on visits since the 1980s, when he would go to garden cafés and casinos and find hundreds of young men and women sitting in couples, talking and whispering for hours on end? He remembered how he once went to Café Granada in Heliopolis to finish reading a book and found dozens of young men and women occupying seats from four o'clock until after six (which was when he left) without renewing their orders or going any further than holding hands. When he asked people they explained that they must be some of the many lovers and fiancés who didn't have anywhere intimate to meet. They could spend years like this, on chairs in cafés or public gardens, whispering and planning to buy an apartment, which would be to accomplish the impossible. How did these lovers and fiancés discover each other's bodies? Such things were delayed because of tradition and the lack of any means to acquire a refuge where they might quench their thirst. Even resorting to a spot at the foot of the Pyramids required owning a car.

Hammad related what he had seen in Café Granada to an Egyptian friend. The friend said, "It seems you as a student only knew the Cairo that Ihsan Abd al-Quddous and Yusuf al-Siba'i write about. There are girls around now whose behavior is way ahead of the romantic adventures in Abd al-Quddous and al-Siba'i. The specimens you saw in Café Granada are wretched people entertaining vain hopes they might realize in ten or more years. Sometimes they've already entered middle age and turned to porn films and magazines like *Playboy*. What happens? In the best case they have a life like that of the family that Sonallah Ibrahim writes about in his novel *Zaat*. I'm sure you've read it. . . ."

Hammad continually thought about the image of the male and female in Arab society, that is the outward appearance, ideas, and feelings that each formed of the other and how close these were to real relationships, and the image that foreign visitors took away of Arab society. When he recalled what he saw in Cairo and Morocco, it seemed to him that male and female images were always presented though a veil. Men were usually good at making themselves look virtuous, masculine and honorable, and condemning of adultery and moral depravity. It was not enough to actually be virtuous; more important was to appear so, whether male or female, and to act like you upheld what people considered virtuous. Women were hallowed in the sanctuary of the family, but on the street they could be contemptible whores. Love was only recognized after engagement ceremonies or during the phase of childhood innocence. How could we arrive at an image that embodied how men and women felt toward one another in a relationship of flesh, blood, and words? Hammad wondered. And how could that image be free from models and illusions based on a one-dimensional desire and lust? In the past the images that Arab society presented of its men and women were censored, especially when disclosing their natural instincts and debauchery. Now the images had amassed and piled atop one another, aboard industrial satellites and international television stations, and the veil had become complex, though it still flooded the imagination and unconscious, and censorship could not stop it. The male resided in the female imagination in the image of the ambiguous and necessarily multifaceted male "other," while the female had begun to occupy the body and imagination of the Arab male through the images of the 'perfect women' that he accumulated from the big or small screen—bold, adulterous, and elegant. The image war's machine gun was leveled to prevent an image of the male and female in Arab society being created that had any connection to that complicated phenomenon called reality.

Hammad's meditations spread into the sphere of fictional art and its role in drawing the features of the image that appeared in shadowy outline before him. Before refractory women's writings appeared, it was the Arab man who controlled discourse, presenting the image of men and women within a didactic or sentimental framework or from a limited perspective because of the need to observe taboos. There was rarely any opposition to these taboos, which made life wretched for men and women and hindered the gradual, parallel discovery of other truths in the collective imagination, the dreams and desires of the individual, and the folds of life. Red lines were always drawn to prevent one from plunging into the labyrinths of the body and soul to probe pain or unearth joys that were searching for a space free from curbs and shackles. The prevailing image in this kind of creativity was emasculated.

Hammad continued his meditation: this was why there was a violent reaction when texts appeared that dealt with sex, men and women, and desire as self-contained elements interacting and competing within a system of complex values in which the common imagination is blended with the individual imagination and with fiction that alters and creates new images. He still remembered how the censors interfered when Sonallah Ibrahim published *The Smell of It*, which portrayed deprivation, repression, and contempt through complex images that combined material description with a poetic delving of the vicissitudes of human relationships. He remembered *Season of Migration to the North* by Tayeb Salih, which awarded sex its full weight in defining behavior and attitudes, and the restrictions placed on the novel in various parts of the Arab world, and likewise on Muhammad Choukri's *For Bread Alone*. He remembered Layla Baalabaki's novel *I'm Alive*, in which a woman ventures to portray her body and soul joining together to reject the lust of an egotistical man. But in truth, the power of censorship could not reach every space, and young authors still managed, with high walls behind them, to convey their lust, despair, and rejection of emasculation and "sleeping in honey."

Hammad remembered being engrossed in this question for a long time and trying to find, in what he read, analyses that might relieve his anxiety and confusion. He was drawn to existentialism and its insistence on creating the essence through responsible freedom, but the importance of personal choice that this involved did not fit well with the weight of other elements determining relationships, behavior, and destiny. Marxism was not particularly interested in carnal appetites and issues relating to sex because it regarded them to be incidental to the fundamental problem of capitalist exploitation and class society. Reich's account of Marxist marriage and the sexual revolution remained an impossible dream. Mao Zedong, in his 'cultural revolution,' wrote instructions about resisting physical desire while he was himself sleeping with carefully acquired lovers, as his personal doctor revealed after his death.

What was this lust that set impulses ablaze and induced men to kill women, or vice versa? How did it rise up sometimes and transform them into forces of giving and innovation?

Hammad liked to follow his meditations, conjuring up relationships, ambiguous and transparent, that he had experienced and pondered the possibility of devising a sociological and ethnological chart to describe and survey the behavior of individuals in Arab society in this lively and extremely complex area. But were detailed field studies able to explain all the surprises and infatuations that kindle fires between men and women? Was it love and sex that drew them together or a complex fantasy that would be difficult to define? He sat amazed one day in front of the television, watching a documentary about love and desire after seventy: dozens of old men and women were meeting in private clubs in France to dance the tango, enjoy themselves, socialize, exchange kisses, and talk about their new adventures during retirement. Hammad recalled a friend who had entered his eightieth year but still loved the company of women. His gray mustache would tremble and his eyebrows would dance in rapture as he greeted the wives of friends and placed two kisses on their feminine cheeks.

Hammad tried to calm his anxiety and sought refuge in things he had read, saying to himself: Perhaps we are, after all, as one English novel says, just "characters in one of God's dreams." Yet these days we seemed to be adapting to the dreams and inventions of video games and the internet. Hammad was baffled when he read recently about the heroine Lara Croft, who was a star of the small screen but not a human being of flesh and blood. A virtual star created from digital units, she played the hero in a video game called "Tomb Raider" and had a woman's face, swelling breasts, and enticing body, and moved about and entered into battles with her enemies on the computer screen. Most important of all, she wouldn't grow old like other film and television stars. She performed, on our behalf, things we couldn't do ourselves, as she took on the identity of the person who moved her with the controller and sent her to ancient Egyptian monuments and Indian tombs in their place. She was not a real person but played the same roles as an actress might. The English inventors of this character declared that their next goal was to introduce human moods into video games, having created virtual human characters. So these games would be the novels of the future. Some people viewed Lara Croft as the harbinger of an army of virtual people, who were waiting at the door and had begun to steal in and occupy a prominent place in our lives. But for the time being Lara stirred hysteria on the small screen, where people remodelled the star's "conventional" image through electronic tricks, removing her clothes and allowing their fantasies to tumble onto her naked body.

As he watched and read about the beings with virtual power inundating the world of actual beings, Hammad thought: The intermingling of these two worlds isn't achieved through flesh, blood, and semen, but through the image. A stream of images creates a phantasmagoria directly, without distance, modification, or sight. It was exciting but frightening. Or rather it was frightening for those committed to what is known as 'human emotion,' despite the ambiguity of the term. Hammad thought ironically: But maybe these virtual beings hold the solution to sex, honor, virginity, and the desire to appear virtuous. There could be solitude without mental suffering and they would sit well with the segregated future to which people are being led by societies that watch and censor and by media entrenched for solitude and emasculation.

Hammad cast a look over what he wrote in his diary on a recent trip to Cairo:

The fundamental and painful thing in any experience of love is the loaded effort required to recreate words, caresses, and things seen. And then there is the plunging into the depths to break free from everything that makes things seem ordinary and repetitive. Without this effort and recreation of the moment, it is not possible to erect love's tent amid the midday heat to protect us from monotony, debasement, and the decline of the body and soul. Perhaps the price of being captivated through the kindling of inner joy is that we lose ourselves (perish?) in unearthing the other and retrieving the self hidden behind the ordinary and acquired.

Hammad smiled and said to himself: If Lara Croft read these words she would be surprised by the sentiments of the 'virtual' beings who lived before her on the face of the earth.

Turnings

HAMMAD AND HIS FRIENDS laughed a lot that evening, and he still laughed whenever he recalled the episode. They were standing at the door of the North African Students' Club watching a formal inspection being carried out by two Egyptian secret police officers on North African students coming to a public gathering for the re-election of the organizing committee. The first rally had been stopped because of violent disputes and harsh words exchanged between the Independents and Baathists. The presence of security representatives the second time round was unavoidable so that clashes were not repeated. Hammad was standing with Barhum and the singer al-Mazkaldi, following the inspection and talking among themselves. After a little while, a friend of theirs, K.S., arrived frowning. His face was draped in a veil of extreme seriousness and he was clutching his right armpit as though hiding something. It was this that attracted the police officer's attention. He shoved his hand into his armpit and pulled out a long knife wrapped in the yellow paper that butchers use to wrap up meat. There was a moment of pushing and shoving during which the officer got hold of the knife.

"What's this?" he demanded.

The student remained silent, his anger preventing him from speaking. Meanwhile the voice of the singer rang out behind the police officer: "Leave him. It's his view he carries in his hand!" he sang cheerfully.

Laughter broke out and the students inside the club came out to watch the incident. The jokes flowed until the rally began.

From 1957 a Baathist cell spreading a different message, inspired by slogans of freedom, unity, and socialism, appeared among the ranks of the Moroccan students. Although their numbers were small, stilted reform in Morocco had opened the way for criticism of the Independence Party, which did not know how to implement the improvements it had promised the people and preferred to enter negotiations and treaties with the palace. Even among the students, most of whom belonged to the Independence Party, there were voices of protest and calls to take up radical positions. However, the prevailing opinion tended toward effecting change from within the party, for there were loyal forces among both the opponents and the unions. Reports began arriving from Morocco of a movement to renew the party under al-Mahdi Benbaraka, who held fast to the basic reforms and was more open to the socialist movement.

Hammad was always at a loss—even decades after—to define why he remained tied, in terms of political preferences, to Moroccan nationalism and its left-wing extensions. There were other attractive options: Nasserism conveyed in the voice of its leader, Baathism with its literature, slogans, and the dynamism of the Arab student cells affiliated to it, and Marxism, at a basic level, through some of the writings he had read out of curiosity.

Now, as he tried to philosophize his reply to this question, his memory took him back to the end of his childhood, when he lived in Rabat and friends of the Independence Party began visiting Muhammad V Independent School and talking to pupils about the imperative struggle for freedom from the French protectorate and the role of Arabic education in preserving identity, memory, and a common history. He remembered well playing soccer in an alley in Rabat and his friends automatically stopping when they saw a short guy with a fierce look on a bike, circling slowly and scrutinizing everything in his path. "Al-Mahdi Benbaraka," they all whispered, and he greeted them with a gentle smile.

Al-Mahdi went on riding his bike for a long time until the French administration banished him to south Morocco. Hammad gradually discovered his political and cultural significance when he began reading his articles in the journal *Risalat al-Maghreb*. He was glad to be connected to a great hand whose movements and activity were overseen by an ordinary guy who went about the alleys and lanes, attended school events, and talked to people on the streets.

In the summer of 1958 Hammad returned to Morocco during the holiday. He got in touch with his friend Fatah and told him that a Young Independents' Conference was going to be held in Tangiers and Benbaraka would be attending.

The atmosphere in Morocco that summer was tense and agitated. There was discontent within the party because the declaration of independence had not granted responsibility to those who deserved it, feudal lords and traitors were still enjoying what they had looted, the demand for constitutional monarchy had faded into the background, and the rituals and customs of the Makhzan (the government finance department) continued to reign arbitrarily. Most attendants at the conference were students studying abroad. General ferment. Awkward questions. Exhausted patience. Haste for reform. Hammad remembered the session chaired by the leader Allal al-Fassi at which al-Mahdi spoke. There was total silence and necks craned in anticipation for what al-Mahdi would say, especially as several reports had been spreading about his disagreements with the leader. Al-Mahdi talked in his special brand of Arabic that mixed classical and colloquial, emphasizing certain letters and moving his hands about while his eyes fixed on the audience. He began with the period of struggle and sacrifices then turned to the roots of the crisis and explained the reasons for the activists' discontent. When he came to the differences among the leadership he basically said, "We are not prophets inspired with perfect judgment. We disagree and strive and disagreement is natural. But it is the cause and questions of the future that define our work. When Allal was exiled in Gabon or was living in Cairo, good coordination was not always possible. We worked hard and were often consistent. Now we are in another phase and must build a new Morocco."

Al-Mahdi, with his experience, ambition, and political and intellectual openness, articulated things that were trembling vaguely in the hearts and minds of the youth at the time. Politics for him, before anything else, was constant reform and clearing the way for everyone to be educated and achieve results through action. His capacity to work ceaselessly was supported by his great reformist sentiment. When he came to Cairo—perhaps for the first time—in 1959, he surprised journalists with his unusual dynamism. Hammad remembered that an Egyptian journalist told him with astonishment about the appointment al-Mahdi had arranged for him at one o'clock in the morning in the café at the Semiramis Hotel because his diary was full and it was the only time he had free.

Perhaps Hammad's special symbolic bond with the Nationalist Movement from when he entered the Arabic education system and participated in demonstrations before the age of ten, then hung around with classmates who set up a guerilla cell in 1954 . . . perhaps this was the umbilical cord that bound him to the grand dream that was seeking to be realized inside him and refused to be the guest of any plan without roots in his childhood or adolescence. Al-Mahdi and others convinced him that political activity was gambling on powers with common roots embedded in the people, as well as, and in particular, a conviction in the necessity of developing ideas and beliefs through practice.

However, when Hammad was older and began to reflect occasionally on what he had seen, he was no longer convinced by this explanation. The past now seemed to him full of gaps, which no one, not even a scrupulous historian, could fill in a manner that satisfied rational logic. Historical action involved responding to a dream which appeared dimly to start with and then interacted with a collective vision to determine the realm of activity and action and to plant in the soul the temptation to change things and relationships, or at least try to improve them. After the experience and conclusion of momentous and important events, we listen to those who played a part in, or witnessed, the action but we aren't carried away by enthusiasm and conviction, because the original components of the dream—which were present as the action developed—are not there in their testimonies and explanations. To penetrate the depths of historical actions, we thus need a record of the dreams of the people who participated in them. If they had recorded their dreams, in their chaos and confusion, and the path that they interrupted to unite in the collective vision and other expectations, it would be possible to grasp the life behind the action. Al-Mahdi died in his prime; they stopped his journey and deprived him of the fighter's rest, when he could have recorded the seeds of the grand dream.

Hammad realized, at first only vaguely, that his dream, even if connected to his birthplace and this outburst of action, opened onto other horizons. His journey to Cairo was part of a dream wrapped up in language, cinema, the Nile, Nasser's revolution, Cairo University, and characters from books and songs. He was enchanted by Nasser and his speeches, especially after the nationalization of Suez and his steadfastness in the face of the Tripartite Aggression. Even so, Nasser's political reforms, embodied by the Arab Socialist Union, were not able to convince or bend public opinion. The experiment of teaching Arab nationalism as a subject in university failed because it talked about an abstract notion in rhetorical, idealized language. It seemed to Hammad that most of the Egyptian students who supported Nasser did not have that much political feeling and rallied around the Union because it was to their benefit. Nasserism was strong in Gamal's speeches and postures, but pallid in the writings of commentators and journalists and in political magazines.

Hammad remembered returning to Cairo in the spring of 1964 to take part in a television training course organized by UNESCO. His longing for the meadows of his youth was still strong and his yearning for Nile casinos was indescribable. But he had experienced several events in Morocco, read new books, and acquired a distance that permitted him to adopt a critical view of the Egyptian society he loved and whose political experiment he followed assiduously and eagerly. Thanks to the UNESCO grant he was able to spend a month enjoying Cairo. He spent evenings with old friends: Farouq Abd al-Qadir, Ahmad Hijazi, al-Bayyati, and Muhammad Awda, whom he had met on his visit to Morocco in 1962. He had read in French Anwar Abd al-Malak's book in French criticizing Nasserism and other studies exposing the fragility of the political experiment in Egypt. On that trip to Cairo he was nursing a deep wound as a result of the suppression to which his party had been subjected in Morocco during the summer of 1963 and a series of judicial proceedings against activists. Many of his friends were behind bars or in exile and everything seemed pointless. There were many questions in his mind and he had serious doubts about the party's decisions, secret reforms, and vision of change. When he met with friends he seemed more radical and unconvinced of the blessings of the leader. He remembered meeting Muhammad Awda in a café after watching the play *Food for Every Mouth* by Tawfiq al-Hakim, having read Awda's piece praising the play. He did not agree with what Awda had written, for the play was oversimplified and reduced socialist equality to a clichéd and pedagogic description. He did not like al-Hakim's recent plays and preferred new writers at the time, like Nu'man Ashour, Alfred Faraj, and Mikhail Roman. He felt that the ramifications of the 1952 Revolution were finally beginning to unfold in the 1960s, despite the walls erected by Nasserism to prevent diversity and difference and to control the powers on the left through absorption and marginalization. A different consciousness was feeling its way, but the personality of the giant leader forced everything back into the bottle so that any resistance or anger had to take place in locked rooms and secret gatherings, until the walls collapsed in 1967 to reveal the debris of a ruined authoritarian regime.

After that visit Hammad began to think about the organization to which he belonged and its political experiment in Morocco, following Nasser's experiment, which seemed to shape its horizon. The illusion was no longer possible or convincing: the spirit of overthrow, the higher revolution, and the slogans asserting historical necessity were dispersed. Defeat in politics did not mean the 'victory' of the adversary and the spread of his power and repression. Rather, it was defeat before the present, which asked for everything except lies wrapped in nostalgia for the past and dreams of the future. The defeat of a policy or of politicians was always before the present.

Hammad would constantly remember his encounter in the early 1970s with the poet Salah Jahin. Hammad had come to Cairo to gather sources relating to his university research and decided to stay in a pension near Qasr al-Nil Street. One night, stretched out on his bed, his ears were flooded with the beautiful melodies of a lute accompanied by a melodious voice and, from time to time, the sound of talk and laughter. It seemed that the people in the room next door were having a social gathering. When he asked the pension owner the next morning who was next door she said it was the composer Sayed Mikkawi. As Hammad was going out in the afternoon he bumped into Salah Jahin at the door and recognized him from his picture. He said hello and introduced himself and they plunged into a spontaneous conversation about poetry, art, and literature. He expressed his wish to get together for longer and Salah Jahin welcomed the invitation and they arranged to have dinner. Though he was depressed, Hammad could still at this time explode with enthusiasm and he still believed in the possibility of a fundamental revision of the Arab Left experiment. Nasser had died, leaving a void that no one knew how to fill. Hammad became youthful and heedless as he criticized and indicated the way forward. Salah Jahin yielded to his conversation partner and made do with interrupting him from time to time to draw his attention to successive failures and retreats and the death of the grand dream.

There was an indescribable sorrow in Salah Jahin's voice. Even when he joked, his feeble laughter could not pierce the sadness that engulfed him. After dinner he insisted on accompanying Hammad to the door of the pension. The conversation continued to pour forth from Hammad's mouth and Salah listened patiently until they arrived at the pension door. Then he said to him frankly, "Listen Ustaz Mohamed, your talk is all very good but alas, it's useless."

"Why Ustaz Salah?"

"Because this nation is essentially right-wing!"

Hammad was surprised by the last remark. He studied Salah's face and saw it draped in a sad look. Then suddenly he roared with laughter and Hammad quickly joined in. They embraced and parted. It was the first and last time Hammad would meet Salah Jahin.

Remaining optimistic and hopeful amid overwhelming suffering and successive failure is not easy. Perpetual pain robs people of hope. The poet who said these words to Hammad on that wonderful evening had himself written dozens of songs and poems challenging the aggressors and celebrating the determination of the Egyptian people. Hammad recalled dozens of Egyptian friends who had spent years in prison or exile then resumed life, still clinging to their right to resist and strive for a better society. Who knew what went on in the mind of a man who had witnessed from the inside the collapse of a beautiful dream and the exuberance, outburst, and happiness it produced?

When Hammad reflected on what he had seen in Egypt or Morocco and the political milieu, there often seemed to be a veil obstructing details of the scene and its complex background. The political idea, as he knew it, leaned on a particular ideal, which was wrapped in grand slogans—liberation, socialism, and democracy—and aligned with models realized in other regions and presented as exemplary. It didn't matter if a decade or two went by and the image remained the same, for the path of the struggle was long and the conditions matured with history, which was sometimes slow but did not lag behind those who believed in it.

When Hammad visited Paris in the summer of 1968 he sensed that a violent wind had swept through France and Europe and rocked its traditional democratic political foundations. What was new in this gust was that it returned people to the core of the political idea and to action. There had, of course, been philosophical writings and analyses throughout the 1960s questioning and casting doubt on liberal society, but the gust of 1968 was unprecedented because it spread the ideas of George Bataille, Foucault, Marquis de Sade, Jean Genet, and others over a wider sphere. Hundreds of youth, students, and workers discussed issues of sexuality, power, and the purpose of life day and night. Why should people continue accepting an idolized system that venerated doctrines, leaders, and ideologies at the expense of the common man, who wanted to enjoy his life on earth and create his destiny in the here and now, removed from the gospels, scriptures, and religious teachings that brainwashed him and paralyzed his imagination, rendering him merely a small nail in a huge arsenal that crushed humanity for the sake of profit and power—profit and power that benefited only a few liberals, communists, socialists, and modern-day medievalists?

During that visit Hammad attended a seminar on female emancipation organized by the Association of North African Female Students in France. He found himself confronted with a new discourse, far from generalizations, ready-made conclusions designed to press where it hurts, and questions springing from the active self. He was delighted to hear these female voices challenging what he was used to hearing from politicians, who dissolved the issue of women into broader issues of society. The spirit of the summer of 1968 was present in the interruptions and questions, and confirmed a profound political concept that had spread from the university realm into the public domain thanks to the demonstrations and debates of May 1968: that politics is not confined to issues of government, the application of laws, and reproducing dominant values through repeated discourses. Rather, it is essentially exposing and determining the dynamics of power, the nature of relationships, and the place of the citizen in the social contract. Thus it was not permissible, as was the case in Hammad's party and the parties of the Arab Left, to break up the issue and freeze some of its components on the pretext that the time wasn't yet right, and to confine oneself to a course that wasn't aimed at altering behavior, relationships, and thinking. The questions of May 1968 broadened the concept of revolution and demanded it be related to people's daily lives, rejecting sanctification, absolutes, and taboos. It was not possible to rely on reason—the selfsame reason that gave us fascism and nazism—divorced from feeling, imagination, and the body.

However, it would become clear to Hammad during his time living and studying in Paris at the beginning of the 1970s that the gust of 1968, with its writings and the activity surrounding it, was more an ideal than reality, for the structures of liberal bourgeois society were deeply rooted and evolving technologically, economically, and electronically. It was these economic structures that would recover citizens' 'faculties of reason' from the expanses of their imagination and return them to the slow democratic struggle. Still, many things had changed in politics, society, and culture, as would become clear in the 1980s in a complicated dialectic that aimed at rooting questions and attitudes.

When Hammad recalled the period between Nasser's death and the assassination of al-Sadat, he did not know what to make of this decade, in which phenomena that noticeably contradicted the slogan of infitah and democracy pronounced in the addresses of the "leader of believers" had come to light: the dozens of millionaires, most of them under fifty, the swelling gap between the poor majority and excessively rich minority, the arrest of figureheads of democratic politics, thought, and literature, and the appearance of radical religious organizations and with them a language of violence. Did all this emerge in a single decade?

Last year, when Hammad was returning to Paris from Cairo, an Egyptian specialist who worked for UNESCO sat next to him on the airplane. They discussed Egypt's circumstances and problems and the specialist, who had been visiting his hometown, spoke of his despair, for the Egypt he saw on his visit was not the one he had dreamed of thirty years ago. Everything he saw bespoke decline. Hammad drew attention to the difficult times and the general Arab predicament but the Egyptian specialist was steadfast in his sorrow. "How long will we wait? We lack the basis for a process of change that can administer the social struggle and restore value to the citizen. I saw several groups operating at different speeds with different ideas and behaviors, side by side but not speaking. People communicate with each other and the state these days through corruption and violence or telephone and television. I can't live in my home country anymore and my children won't be able to bear it."

Hammad went back to looking out of the airplane window at the land they were leaving behind. The words of the man sitting beside him reminded him of similar discussions he had heard during his visit. He recalled a passage he read the night before in a Japanese novel that embodied the daily "bloody struggle" into which Egyptians plunged: "They're all on fire. There isn't a coward among them pushing them to save themselves. They snatch what they can from life just as men and women snatch moans of pleasure in bed then confront death with the same rigor, dreaming of building a new world."

When Hammad learned of the death of Sayed Mikkawi he remembered the evening when he listened to his neighbor's voice in the pension, and then afterward followed his beautiful songs: "The Night of Birth," "The Rubiyyat," "Yesterday I Could Not Sleep". . . . He put on a tape and immersed himself in listening and reflecting. The voice of Sayed Mikkawi rang out: "Union is always precious. . . ." He remembered him and Salah Jahin. He recalled the gestures, features, words, laughter, and sighs. He felt that he shared a special space with these two men, created in his memory on that visit to Cairo at the beginning of the 1970s. The encounter was brief but an intimate bridge had been woven between them. They were dead but he was still alive, listening to the songs of one and reading the poems of the other. He wondered: what do you call a relationship that connects you with an invisible thread to worlds that overwhelm and flood your emotion?

During days of banality and lies Hammad was beset by feelings of feebleness and disgust at belonging to an ocean without a horizon, submerged in blindness. He would remember Salah Jahin, whom he only knew for a couple of hours but who had displayed a piercing insight, for his predictions had increasingly proved true with the successive gray days. It seemed to Hammad that Salah had been speaking to him from a different place and that this accorded him critical perception, courage, and the ability to ignore the philosophers: perhaps this place was the world of the dead, a world he seemed to be associated with after being overtaken by constant depression and sadness.

Hammad's mind roamed freely amid songs and memories. He said to himself: Was this reminiscing connected to that thing buried in the depths of childhood and adolescence that guides us when we are about to open up to others through politics? Was it the same thing that accompanies us when we rush into the thick of action spurred on by a mirage of changing the existing reality?

Whenever Hammad turned a year older he became more convinced that the question of choice at the beginning of youth could not be answered directly or fully. The answer harbored fixed seeds and others that evolved and emended the original idea. "Turnings" resembled moments harmonized within variation.

Part Two
Extending the Thread of Memory

When Osiris suddenly appeared—for the niche was cut right into the wall—under the green light, I was scared. Were my eyes, naturally, informed first? No. First my shoulders and the back of my neck, crushed by a hand or a mass that compelled me to sink into the Egyptian ages and, mentally, to bow down and even to crouch before this tiny statue with its hard gaze, its hard smile. Here indeed was a god. Of the inexorable. (I am speaking, as may have been realized, of the figure of Osiris standing in the crypt of the Louvre.) I was scared because no mistake was possible: this was a god.

—Jean Genet, "The Studio of Alberto Giacometti"

The Honey
of Zagazig

I ARRIVED IN CAIRO, this time at six in the morning, with some
friends, having just attended a conference together in Baghdad
in solidarity with the Palestinians confined in Tall al-Zaatar
at the end of August. We headed to the Hilton Hotel but were
told we would have to wait until nine o'clock when some of
the guests were leaving. We left our bags and went out to walk
around and look for a café. Cairo was almost empty. The clean-
ers were going round with water hoses spraying the roads and
the first minibuses and newspaper sellers were arriving in Tahrir
Square. I was longing for Cairo after a tense few months and the
conference, which had stuffed us full of speeches and slogans
and increased our sense of impotence. At least in Cairo I could
meet friends and sit on the banks of the Nile, and melt into the
vast space and the temporary repose that the anonymity granted.
Some of my companions were visiting Cairo for the first time.
I suggested that we go to al-Fatatri on Bab al-Luq's main street

and talk about everything, and that we visit some of the historical sites and telephone our mutual friends in the evening. They agreed but were tired and waiting for the rooms to sleep a little, then everything was possible. After breakfast we went to Café Astra, bought papers and immersed ourselves in discussing the news. The time passed slowly. There were not enough rooms for all of us so I said I could make my own arrangements. I telephoned a Moroccan friend, Isam, who had stayed in Cairo after I left. He came with the key to an empty flat in Bab al-Luq. I slept until afternoon and when I awoke the city had recovered its usual noisy rhythm; the minarets were broadcasting Qur'anic recitations, the radios blaring out songs, programs, and open discussions. I liked the flat, though it was in a very old building with a balcony overlooking Huda Shaarawi Street. The windows had green wooden frames and their proximity to those of the neighbors created the impression of intimacy and close community. The flat had two rooms. One was an assorted library made up of series from the publisher al-Hilal, my book, al-Hilal novels, and hundreds of works of history, literature, and politics. The other contained a bed and small table. It was a picture that spoke a thousand words. My friend rarely went there but would let passing friends use it. I made tea and began thinking about a plan for the evening with my companions, who only had two days before they traveled on to Morocco. I was intending to stay for two weeks, as I loved Cairo and because I had an errand to undertake on behalf of a friend, who had met a teacher at a conference in Alexandria the year before and given me some books for her. You'll be able to communicate with her more than I could because you speak Egyptian, he had said to me. I telephoned her right away. Sayyida Saniya made charming conversation. She asked about our friend and said she was happy to make my acquaintance. We arranged to meet in two days time. I waited for her at Groppi's as agreed. She was attractive and had an air of coquettishness about her. We talked in French a little as she was learning it. She asked me about my student days in Egypt and my interests, and friendship began to weave close threads between us. Just as my friend had said, there was discord between her and her husband, who worked in commerce while she had a job at a research institute and was interested in culture and literature and wanted to publish. At the time I was living on impulse and ready to go wherever my appetite and discoveries took me. I spontaneously invited her to dinner at the flat and afterward to see one of Muhammad Subhi's plays. She wavered a little but I encouraged her as a modern woman who could not refuse the invitation of an admirer who was alone in Cairo, especially as her husband was away. So she came. Her eyes sparkled and her conversation was sweet. She was in full blossom. I sensed that she wanted to prove that she was able to lead her own life. She still wasn't getting on with her husband and the interests of their two families still stopped them from separating, which prevented her from living as she wished, especially as she clung to the model of female emancipation that she beheld when she visited Europe with her father. Nevertheless, she resisted my flirting and the lust that gradually made itself known. She complained to me about my friend, who had not understood her openness when they met at the conference in Alexandria. I told her that I was made from different clay: he studied in France and all his relationships were casual.

"What about you?" she asked.

"As you can see, weak in the face of kindness, a tanned complexion, and eyes promising warmth."

Gradually our lips met and our bodies moved closer. As we approached orgasm her eyes filled with tears and she wept while our bodies convulsed. I kept quiet until the blood in our arteries had calmed. Then I wiped her tears and asked what was wrong, but she didn't know. Was it her inner anxieties? Or had liberating her body reminded her of the past and of social conventions and the punishments of the shari'a and religious judges?

She calmed down and we resumed our frenetic, happy chatter. I insisted that we go and watch the play. I can't remember the title but I remember Muhammad Subhi's talents and skillful body, as supple as rubber. We burst into laughter as he stretched his cheeks and jaw and twisted his body and delivered lines that made the audience crack up. Suddenly a spectator sitting in the front row began heckling him. He shot back one or two sharp remarks, which we laughed at, but the insufferable spectator persisted with his insipid attacks and the troupe was forced to lower the curtain. Someone came out and convinced the spectator to withdraw after some yelling and shouting.

Saniya and I stayed in touch for a while. We would meet up when I visited Cairo and our relationship evolved into a friendship. Sometimes I felt that she was submerged in a swamp of family and professional problems. At the institute they threatened to fire her because she was in a hurry to publish and plagiarized several pages from a study in English, while with her husband she continued to perform the role that severed her from herself, lacking the courage to lead the life she desired. There was also the glowing image of her successful father, who spoiled her and puffed her up and pushed her to excel though she possessed neither the wings nor the courage. When her father died she was lonely and afraid. She was overcome with regret about her married life. She began to withdraw into a tent of repentance and her suffering continued. It isn't pretty to find a woman in a state of fear, having known her shining with dreams of ascent and conquering the world.

Did It
Really Happen?

I SEEM TO REMEMBER, as we were sitting in Café Astra on Tahrir Square that morning waiting for the hotel, that I saw the poet Amal Dunqul sitting in the corner. I had never met him before but recognized him from his picture in the paper. He was having coffee with someone and leafing through the papers. As we left I stopped at his table, introduced myself, and expressed the wish to interview him that week. He was quiet and a deep sadness enveloped his wide eyes. I took my leave and rejoined my companions, and was swept into the whirlpool. I never came across Amal Dunqul again.

Perhaps that evening was spent at the house of Farida and Hussein Abd al-Raziq. I'm not certain but I think we got to know them through mutual friends in the political sphere and Hussein's frequent visits to Morocco in those days. But I don't remember anything about the evening. I remember that while I was waiting for Sayyida Saniya in the apartment in Bab al-Luq I put a lot

of effort into dusting, chasing the cockroaches out of the bath-
room, and cleaning the dining table in the main room. Perhaps I
called Amm Sulayman and asked him to fetch drinks and three
bottles of Stella, and instructed him to welcome the journalist
who would be visiting the flat at six o'clock to interview me! I'm
not sure if she wept out loud, as I was too aroused and absorbed
in the moment, but I remember the rest of her tears as we lay on
our backs and I stroked her cheeks with my fingers, then turned
over and embraced her in silence and tried to show how unusual
I was with my lively conversation. Did we have dinner in the
apartment or at Kebabgi al-Geish Street? The theater tickets
we bought were from the black market, no doubt, because the
nine-thirty showing was *complet*. I think that's what happened.
It doesn't matter. I think after we left the theater she insisted
that I ride with her in her car so she could take me around a bit
in Doqqi, Agouza, Zamalek, and along the banks of the Nile.
I was keen on the idea but asked that afterward I could have a
go driving, even though I didn't have a license. She agreed, for
everything we did that night fell into the category of 'refreshing
madness,' which she believed to be the motto of lovers of life
in France. She began repeating "Les Folies Rafraichissantes"
in French for us to use as a passport to our suppressed desires.
When she dropped me off in Bab al-Luq she told me she had to
go to Zagazig, her hometown, the next day. She would be back
in the evening. I asked her about the best thing in her hometown.
"Goodness. Haven't you heard of Zagazig honey?" she asked.

"Not until now!"

I think she phoned me that night at two in the morning to
wish me a good day the next day and I flirted a lot about Zagazig
honey and told her I was on tenterhooks to taste it when she
brought it that evening.

Les Folies Rafraichissantes! What a delight. We used these
words as a motto to sum up our secret desires and to allow us

to collude without the usual restraints. I'm sure we're not the only ones to have used such words to sneak outside fences and sanctuaries. But what can replace the stimulating fragrance that Les Folies Rafraichissantes leave behind when our impulsiveness and vigor dissipate and we enter monotony, composure, and waiting for something that never comes?

Extensions

It returned suddenly. I felt it spread slowly, rising from unknown depths, faster than I thought. I tried in vain to block it. In one go it occupied my esophagus and spread through my cells, smothering my throat and planting tears in my eyes.

I recognized it. I'd experienced it before. Before it was understandable. But now? I sensed it wasn't fleeting like its predecessors. It was a permanent choking then? How could I endure it?

I tried to fool it. I dressed quickly and rushed into the street. I walked quickly, gulping the fresh air. Day was just beginning and the commotion of pedestrians and car horns was growing. I walked without knowing where I was going and after a while found myself at the door of a building. I wasn't conscious of how much time had passed since I'd left the hotel. A large arch, whose engravings I couldn't make out, surrounded the door. Dust. Dirt. Dilapidated steps. The sloping straw chair was in its usual place but was empty.

I climbed the staircase to the third floor and stopped in front of an apartment door covered in layers of dust and grime. I listened a little. Not a sound or noise from behind the glass aperture. The flat next door was also lifeless. I began to descend. At the door I came across a tanned young man wearing a woollen gallabiya. He smiled and raised his hand in greeting. I asked him about the doorman, Amm Sulayman.

"May you live long," he said.

"The apartment on the third floor. Does anyone live there?"

"No. There is an effendi who comes sometimes with his mistress, pardon me. . . . They stay for a bit then go."

The choking sensation was still there. I could feel it spreading and stabbing as I left Bab al-Luq and headed to Tahrir Square and then the Nile. Images, specters, and scenes from the distant and recent past thronged my imagination. It's natural, I said to myself. Entirely natural. It's been more than thirty years. Why do you expect to find things as you left them? And even if you did, what would you do? What would you do with the people? Why can't you accept the changes in yourself and others over time, which never stops moving?

It will go away, I said, deceiving myself. I'll take a boat trip on the Nile. The boatman asked me if I wanted something to drink but I didn't answer. "I have everything. Just say the word," he said. I smiled. I understood what he was intimating but told him that I just wanted him to stray with me on the Nile without talking. The waves competed and the boat rocked. The freshness brushed against me as we moved away from the noise of the traffic and tumult of the city.

I felt it rising again from my intestines and taking hold of my throat, surrounding my eyes with tears locked in the sockets. If only I knew what stirred it this time. I was in good spirits in the heart of the Cairo I love, friends inundating me with affection, feeling alive. So where did the terrible choking feeling come from?

Heart, Look Who's Come

It was a coincidence though it didn't seem that way.

After all that time, after sinking low, getting used to it, adjusting to living in the present as it was and becoming absorbed in the moment with its joys and bitterness . . . the slender, crystalline specter rises up, wearing an innocent, ambiguous smile, with a few clever words to tell you that the heart's doors never close.

But this time it's different. You and her are steeped in social conventions, locked in fences that barely permit your heart to beat and the blood to warm in your arteries, with no hope of communion. The journey brought a surprise after all these years. Cairo was not the place stored in your memory, colored by words and late afternoon breezes burning with the passion of young men. It was as though—despite her radiant youth—she was searching for your Cairo and consulting your memories to penetrate the depths of a city whose mythical features you painted before the journey. The itinerary of travel and living change. Your anguished longing for the past, buried in ruins or buildings and tall offices vaunting their newness, has dispersed. Your desire to return to a bygone time and open your pores to that spectral, exquisitely delicate, femininity has disappeared. Was this the victory of the beautiful present over the past? Or an escape toward illusions that intimate new experiences and a time that never ends?

Heart, look who's come. At the start of each day, before my morning walk around the museums and souqs and seat on the edge of the Nile, the kiss of greeting is innocent and ambiguous. The joining of hands and electric current refreshes our two bodies. Then the journey is resumed with its daily minutiae until evening arrives and the kiss of farewell is repeated, with its ambiguity, spontaneity, and magnetic electricity. Between the two kisses you are happy and cheerful, on the point of finding what you were looking for in the corners of a soul pursuing the spaces of yesterday, trying to fathom what it experienced in haste and exuberance. You are on the point of finding what you came in search of in the expanses of Cairo and the hidden parts of your soul. At night you eagerly surrender to sleep and recall the luminous specter and small breasts dancing under the diaphanous blouse. You say to yourself that these breasts were created thus forever. They won't grow or shrink, but stay as they are, towering bashfully, planted at the fountainhead of harmony in a body possessed of a secret charm.

Three months later I returned to Cairo and she was not with me on the journey. Soon the space, people, and things reclaimed their familiar character in a memory that clung to past images and vanished milieus. Every morning you said that you were not searching for a bygone era; you wanted to be incorporated into a fast-flowing current, from which you could see the past. But you were a stranger now. Your time was consigned to your memory and the memories of some of the people you knew. There was nothing left but to get used to being a visitor opening virgin eyes to see and be surprised and accumulate anew.

Look at this peasant woman in her black gallabiya and embroidered veil standing in front of this wooden plank, supported by bricks, and clay grill covered with ears of corn, her husband or companion sitting to the side, smoking a shisha, from time to time moving the mouthpiece to exchange a few words. She is engrossed in turning the corn. Her face suggests strength and stubbornness and her person fills the place. Cars fly past, horns hooting. You turn into a side street and read the blue sign: "Champollion Street." You proceed, your eyes widening to gather all the details. Why do you dawdle and think back to the first time you came across this street?

There was (there is no avoiding using "was" however hard I try) a little rain drizzling and the December clouds were thickening. You were returning from a long walk carrying books and a striped vest you had bought in Khan al-Khalili. You said, I'll drink some tea before carrying on. You entered the street named after Champollion, whose historic role in deciphering the ancient Egyptian hieroglyphs you had read and heard about. On your left was a local café with some tables and a handful of customers. You sat down in the corner and ordered tea. There were two middle-aged men in front of you, playing dominoes and chatting. After a little while you heard one of them say, looking up at the sky, "The sky is spitting."

Your memory was stirred, for the word *tanda'*—to spit—reminded you of a word in classical Arabic meaning the appearance of the first drop of water or sweat. You smiled and said to him, "The word you just used, sir, is classical."

"Excuse me?"

"I was going to say that *nadha'a* comes from *nadha' al-ma'* to drip water, to come out and become clear."

"Oh, in grammatical Arabic, you mean? Sir, we prefer *tanda'*, which we learn with spoken language. You know we don't ask if a word is classical or colloquial. Tell me, what do you say for *tanda'*?"

"We say the sky is spraying—*tatbukh*—which is an Arabic word too.

"Really. Forgive me, but that means something else for us."

There was laughter and an invitation to tea and chat.

You continue on your way, avoiding memories of yesterday, and trying not to let your eyes stare. Objects and faces pile up. You won't be able to gather up everything you see. Don't trouble yourself. Let what is outside you choose how it dwells in you. These alleys and streets are part of your daily round. You need only pass through and become accustomed to what's before your eyes.

Yet you cannot help remembering what the author of *Prisoner of Love* wrote with his usual shining simplicity: "The present is always hard and the future is even harder. The past, or rather the absent, is worshiped while we live in the present."

Wedding Song or
When a Dead Man
Observes the Living

AT THE BEGINNING OF the 1980s, I was analyzing the novel *Wedding Song* with postgraduate students and noticed that this was the only novel in which Naguib Mahfouz treats the relationship between the author and the fictional world from within the text, interrogating and disturbing the novelist. With the exception of *The Beggar* and *Adrift on the Nile*, which contain indications of the relationship between fiction and reality, the texts of Naguib Mahfouz's novels do not interrogate themselves. The structure of *Wedding Song*, on the other hand, is built on contradictions generated by the dissimilarity and intermeshing of reality and fiction, which creates space for the emergence of suggestive ambiguities, rich in symbols and interpretations. Four characters—Tariq Ramadan, Karam Yunis, Halima al-Kabash, and Abbas Karam Yunis—narrate, each from their own perspective, a set of collective events, which constitute the space that brings together the director of a theater troupe, a group of actors, and a drama

entitled *Wedding Song*, written by Abbas Karam Yunis, son of
Halima and Karam, drawing on the anxiety and turmoil he experienced as a child as he watched the evening gatherings of his parents and their actor friends around a table of gambling, drinking,
and ephemeral entertainment, before his parents were arrested
by the police and sent to jail for a number of years. Because the
son, Abbas Karam Yunis, was close to the theater and enamored
by it, he plunged into writing and discovered the crisis of the
author who seeks inspiration in a burning experience lodged in
his skin and memory. Mahfouz uses this fictional story to write
a multilayered novel, which seems to record the experience of
a dramatist with his text and with the actors who performed the
play on the stage, and before that lived its events in real life.

This is not the place for a detailed analysis of this fine novel,
but I want to pause for a minute at the remarkable moment when
Abbas Karam Yunis, after the success of his first play, decides
to disappear and notify friends that he has committed suicide
because he cannot take the dryness that has settled over him as
a body without a soul. Everyone thinks him dead. But then he
wakes from his slumber and feels he has slept for a whole age
and woken in a new era. So he takes back his suicide, for he per-
ceives a novel fragrance amid the failure and dryness.

In the first instance I saw Abbas Karam Yunis' situation as
representing one of three possibilities in the relationship between
the narrator and fictional character. It represented that rare case,
suggested in theory more often than encountered in a text,
whereby the fictional character knows more than the narrator.
In fact, in *Wedding Song* the play's vanished omniscient author
knows more than the other narrators, who believe he has committed suicide. The playwright is dead but continues to observe
the living as well as himself and his reincarnations.

Later, when I reread the novel, it seemed me to that this character who knows more than the narrator resembles the author, in

a general sense, if the latter is regarded as a dead person observing the living from afar and from a distance that permits him to see clearly and sharply, without ambiguity or flattery. Who other than a dead person can grasp things, relationships, and situations with profound neutrality and perception? Surrounded by silence, the dead observer draws near to the noisy, tangled haze of reality and gathers up that which will restore him to life and restore life to that which appears scattered, dislocated, without symptom or suggestion. For this reason, I consider *Wedding Song* to be Naguib Mahfouz's most modern novel; for it is constructed on a complex dialectic within which elements clash then intermesh, then branch off and open up once more, eliminating the boundaries between reality and imagination, death, and life.

I was intending to use these observations as an introduction to the discussion that I conducted with Naguib Mahfouz in 1989 at the request of the review *Palestinian Studies*, which was published in Paris. But the great writer was tired and worn from the plethora of appointments and interviews with newspapers and television after winning the Nobel prize, so I made do with questions of a general nature, aimed at setting forth the elements of a constructive reading of his novels.

When I arrived in Cairo at the end of 1989, the winter sun I loved was waiting for me, shining at the height of winter and emitting rays that glittered on the surface of the Nile, whose water level had returned to normal after a passing drought. From the biting cold and continuous rain in Rabat and Paris to the festival of warm sun in Cairo. It was a happy migration and an incentive for activity, trailing the twenty-first Cairo International Book Fair, meeting up with friends, and surrendering to Cairene nights.

While I waited for the appointment that Mahfouz had arranged for our chat, I recalled the first time I saw him on the number six bus, which traveled between Ataba and Agouza. I was in my first year at the College of Arts and had begun reading his novels after Taha Hussein commended his talent and ability for description and examining people. I recognized him by the mole beneath his left nostril. He was wearing dark glasses and from time to time I saw him talk and smile with a passenger who had introduced himself. I didn't dare speak to him when I came across him on that bus, but contented myself with following his news in the papers and reading his stories and novels and what was written about him. When I returned to Morocco in the summer of 1960, I continued to read his work and to wait longingly for what his imagination would invent in order to depict some of the evermore tangled and confused threads. The 1960s opened onto a diversity of questions, and the answers were varied and abundant, characterized by confidence and decisiveness. Despite reading a large number of political and ideological works at the time, it was the poems, stories, and novels I read that granted me gulps of fresh air and allowed me to steal into an intimate realm where I detected things that were obscure or had been neglected. The excitement and high spirits did not eclipse shades of fear and anxiety about the future, however. When I read *The Thief and the Dogs* I found that Mahfouz had begun to put out antenna and observe a profound change in the structure of Egyptian society. Perhaps the meanings I would point to were not entirely clear in his mind when he was writing the book, but several things justified talking about the existance of a deep perception in that short, tightly woven text, whose language is characterized by a dense lyricism. In my last year of university I followed the exciting story in the papers of a clever thief called Muhammad Amin Mahmoud Sulayman, whom the press nicknamed "al-Saffah"—the killer—and who gained wide popularity because he attacked the houses and villas of the rich and gave some of the loot to the poor. It was April 1960 and we followed al-Saffah's conquests with the same keenness we would a good television soap opera today. I remember our charming maid Umm Fathiya being excited and happy as she related snippets of what people were saying in her quarter about the thief who humbled the police and awoke fantasies in the imagination of downtrodden Egyptians. "I wish al-Saffah would visit me tonight. How wonderful," she would say. In some popular Egyptian legends, characters like the hero Adham al-Sharqawi, whose exploits involved attacking the rich in the interest of the poor, would meet al-Saffah. But as I was teaching *The Thief and the Dogs* at college from 1961, I began to discover other aspects of the novel, which might be seen as a critical elegy to the romantic Arab illusion that had been growing since the establishment of a state whose legitimacy depended on the nationalist phase and its values of colonial resistance.

Said Mahran in *The Thief and the Dogs* is the voice that announces the death of the dream of harmony between the people and the state. "If someone kills me, they kill millions. I am the dream, the hope, the cowards' redemption. I am the example, the consolation, and the tears that shame a man," he says. But he does not realize that the inevitable smothering that results from sociopolitical restructuring is tantamount to a severance with what went before: the state widened its bureaucratic and social foundations to meet a vital ambition with national dimensions, and it needed intellectuals to support it. Raouf Elwan, the revolutionary of yesterday, becomes a bigmouth who excuses what the political reality imposes on him even though he knows that intellectuals and activists have been thrown into prison. What justice is Said Mahran talking about? His lone voice becomes isolated amid the din of the infernal machines supporting the edifice of the strong national state. Yet he still has the courage to remind people about "pure" fundamental values, without understanding that his voice, however much it kindles the enthusiasm of the poor, will not convince anyone to oppose the abuse and iniquities attending the new structure. Thus Said Mahran's voice remains as strange as the romantic revolutionary in times of practical exigency. It doesn't matter whether the thief kills himself, as happened in real life, or surrenders unconcerned to the police, as Said Mahran does, because the space has been filled with systems, organizations, and institutions that embody the illusion of the powerful new structure in accordance with its accompanying discourses. This illusion would continue until June 1967, though at the time I don't think anyone remembered Said Mahran, the dead man who vowed to observe the living when he raised his voice and drew attention to the cracks in the structure's foundations.

From my return to Morocco in 1960 to the beginning of the 1980s, I continued to read Naguib Mahfouz's stories and novels eagerly, for a secret understanding had been woven between me as a reader and him as an author. As events and failures piled up and horizons were obscured, he always found a way to create narrative spaces that gathered echoes of Egypt's experience and represented it in evermore imaginative ways. In spite of the criticism he faced in the 1950s—that his vision was confined to the oscillating aspirations of the petit bourgeoisie—I found his texts prompted new questions, which emanated from daily life and which he was able to represent symbolically, thus transporting them from the realm of hallucination and miscarriage into the poetic imagination, which in turn enriches the collective, popular imagination. Perhaps his renewed point of departure was an attempt to respond, through novelistic texts, to the questions of his hero in the *Cairo Trilogy*, Kamal Abd al-Gawad: Is there truth and untruth? What is the relationship between reality and what is in our heads? What is the value of history? What is the relationship between Aida the adored, and pregnant Aida? Who am I?

In Rabat, his novels relieved my loneliness and kindled the longing for Egypt that lived inside me. I would immerse myself in reading *Autumn Quail*, *Adrift on the Nile*, *Miramar*, *Karnak*

Café, *Love in the Rain*, *Under the Bus Shelter*, *Fountain and Tomb*, and *The Harafish*. Through them I got used to illusions being dispelled and doubting what was presented as truth and history. When I met him in 1989, I pointed to the shift in the aforementioned novels toward hidden truths. He replied, "None of my novels are without a search for what lies behind reality. It seems to me when I read my novels, or rather when I recall them (for I don't reread them), that I am divided between two interests: a strong interest in reality and questioning in order to uncover the hidden forces behind reality."

He arranged to meet me at half past seven in the morning at Café Ali Baba, where he usually had his coffee and read the papers. He met me smiling and welcoming. The signs of tiredness were clear on his face and his hearing was not as good as when I interviewed him in 1973 at Groppi's. He constantly asked me to repeat myself, putting his hand behind his ear. Because the questions were long and included analytical observations, there wasn't enough time to exhaust them, and he couldn't interrupt his schedule. So he gave me another appointment, two days later, at the same time and place. His answers centered on what he considered fundamental, and when he found the question and observations were close to what he had been aiming for, he said he agreed with what I had said because it contained the answer. He was modest and friendly and it did not seem to me that the international reputation brought to him by the Nobel prize had changed him.

Nevertheless, something in Naguib Mahfouz made me pause and continuously aroused my curiosity. I don't know how to describe it but it began from his novelistic texts and led to his personal life, which he had always been keen to keep sheltered and hidden. This was perfectly natural and his reasons were convincing in a society where the press had an appetite for tearing apart stars and artists. The public image of Mahfouz seemed to be overly judicious and grave, which contradicted the impulsive-ness, pain, burning, and agitation—especially where women, pleasure, and socializing were concerned—that I found in the pages of his stories. However much I sensed a tendency in his writings toward balancing the whims of the body, mysticism of the soul, and exploring people's depths and behavior, his books betrayed an unusual appetite for life and its charms, drawn, it seemed to me, from an adventurous spirit that had undergone the experience and was embroiled in its flames, not confined to transmitting the echoes. I felt that the persistent themes scattered through Mahfouz's novels pointed to a 'hidden wound', which wasn't visible in his biography or the image people had of him, but was present and effective and fed the split between his appe-tite for life and buried sadness. I became sure of this impression as I watched a film on French television about Mahfouz's life in August of 1996. In a beautiful and unexpected scene we see him playing on a qanun, full of youth and vitality. Then we see him when he is older, talking about his novelistic world in terms of the quarter, the futuwwa, and the dancers who fill people's lives with joy and entertainment, then on the Nile with a group of friends famously known as the harafish. A beautiful world that united dualities striving for integration: the futuwwa and dancers symbolized the instinct of violence and struggle next to fun and the pursuit of pleasure. The quarter and the Nile: a closed, self-contained space and a river that flowed and opened up onto for-eign places. As for the harafish and their ritual weekly meetings, they seemed to personify the vagabonds who refused to submit to restrictive social norms. The harafish represented a desire in many people to escape from the clasp of monotony and social conventions, a desire to exist both within society and outside it in order to achieve the balance favored by Mahfouz, as he says in one of his novels: "It is because people need to love the world and, at the same time, free themselves from its slavery." But

119

how? How can we free ourselves from "slavery" to the world and its temptations, especially when we want to live and not to make do with familiar, monotonous existence? When we face the limits of the impossible and are drawn to the realm of death?

Whenever I go to Egypt, I go armed with what my memory has amassed from the literary imagination of Egyptian authors, foremost among them Naguib Mahfouz, who draws on the collective imagination just as he furrows into his own imagination, which watches out for raw narrative breeding abundantly in the quarters, streets, and buildings of Cairo and Alexandria and in everyday conversations. But the three texts I recall most are *The Beggar*, *Wedding Song*, and *The Thief and the Dogs*. It seems to me that there is a delicate thread connecting these three novels, bringing them together at that invisible secret wound, which alternates between rash outbursts and a resigned sadness that withdraws to the calm of death to observe life.

In *The Beggar*, the lawyer Umar al-Hamzawi is used to rock a seemingly solid structure (family, children, struggle in one of the parties of the left) and transport us into the realm of doubt and the chaos of the stricken heart. All the boundaries, attitudes, and values he has lived by are suddenly shaken when a sense of futility sneaks surreptitiously into his soul and being. The doctors are confused as he appears physically healthy, but he feels the worm of anxiety and uselessness deep inside him. Thus he becomes intent on experiencing everything that lies beyond propriety, social conventions, and the contract of marriage. He pursues a remote path of libertinism, sex, and pleasure, perhaps to discover the root of his strange illness. But despite his nocturnal adventures, which are dispersed by the light of morning, his disconnection from the world continues. "If you really want me, why did you abandon me?" he says to the chanteuse. It is as though he is dead among the living. Even when he meets his friend Uthman Khalil, a left-wing activist who has been released from jail after many years, he cannot, like him, recover himself or his warmth. He is surprised by the firmness of his friend the activist, whose beliefs and faith in the future have not weakened, while he—Umar al-Hamzawi—is crushed inside, a body without a pulse or desire. He is a dead beggar among the living, but he longs for death, which might restore his appetite for life and ability to connect with the world.

The value of *The Beggar* is not in its discussion and debate about the superiority of science over art in the era of increasing technology, for this is a familiar issue. Rather it lies in the way that it translates into the Arab imagination the confrontation between nihilism, as a way of life that does not look to greater horizons, and ideological belief, which aspires to change society and the world. Time is no longer progressive, full and positive, as the discourses of the Nahda (nineteenth-century Arab cultural revival) and reform declared it to be, because in the 1960s the citizen discovered that he was worth nothing to the repressive national state and therefore could not be himself. Instead, he was forced into hypocrisy and silence and burying his conscience. Excessively rounded discourse, crammed with ready-made answers, is always at the cost of the discourse of the self and its suppressed desires. Is it the destiny of Arabs to live diminished, wretched, ground down by rules and prohibitions?

In *The Beggar* and other novels by Mahfouz, the social dimension is added to by existential angst, the journey of the self into its infernal depths, and a rebellion against restrictive, vindicating reason. This gravitation to remote situations, especially in *The Beggar*, blends images of society and its manifestations and behaviors with the imaginary in order to modify and broaden the collective, popular imagination. Mahfouz did not shy away from issues like these, buried in the communal unconscious and in need of loosening, as for instance in *Children of the Alley*. But he always anticipated a moral renewal behind a bold creative vision, as he said to me, "Art may sometimes appear to be trying to wreck moral values, but if we look closely it will contain a call for a new morality connected to the needs of society. For example, the poetry of Abu Nuwas, which is usually described as anarchic, calls for a new morality through its appeal for freedom and emancipation from prohibitions."

The last time I met Naguib Mahfouz was on October 10, 1995 in a café on the deck of a small steamer on the banks of the Nile. The suggestion came from his friend Gamal al-Ghitani who, along with Yusuf al-Qaid and a small group of the writer's companions, had become the link between him and the outside world after the attempt on his life. That evening on the boat there were some security men to guard him sitting in a corner. Mahfouz was surrounded by three of his friends and smiled when he received us. His movements were slower than I remembered and his neck tilted forward a little. Al-Ghitani spoke loudly as he introduced us and the conversation was unsteady because a 'translation' of everything into a loud voice required some effort. Following its usual ritual, the gathering began with a summary of important news, events, and cultural activities, offered alternately by al-Qaid and al-Ghitani. Mahfouz listened with his hand on his ear, occasionally asking for clarification or commenting briefly. Gradually his sharp insight and capacity for irony and humor returned. There was news of the parliamentary elections and the struggles in which government departments, parties and certain names were involved. Suddenly Mahfouz asked, "Isn't Sayyida Fayrouz going to be nominated for any department?" His familiar laugh reverberated amid our laughter. Then his smiles darkened as he listened and his face seemed wrapped in an unmistakable bitterness. His charm that evening made me forget his difficult mental and physical circumstances, for his mind was as sharp as ever, astute and shining with ironic and humorous remarks, reminiscent of gatherings on the houseboat in *Adrift on the Nile*.

Someone told him that letters were being sent by citizens every day to the mosque of Gamal Abd al-Nasser. "Has anyone read them?" Mahfouz asked. The speaker replied that he didn't know. "Maybe the letters are to complain about him and his evils, since no one was able to while he was alive!" said the writer.

Amid the laughter and seriousness, I seized the opportunity to say to him, through the voice of al-Ghitani, that readers in Morocco had been deprived of reading *Echoes of an Autobiography*, which was published as a series in *al-Ahram*, and that I hoped he would permit it to be published as a book. He apologized that the text had been published "mixed up" because his weak eyesight after he was attacked had not permitted him to review what he had written. Al-Ghitani grabbed the chance to suggest that he and someone else take responsibility for editing the text and publishing it in *Akhbar al-adab*, which regularly reached Morocco. Mahfouz agreed so long as it was published in two parts, not one.

The time for him to take his medication approached so we said goodbye to the great writer and he agreed that we could take some photographs to remember the occasion. He was friendly and enduring of the fate that dictated how he organized his time and came between him and his writing and reading. I suspected that he felt some bitterness toward his circumstances, which stopped him continuing his simple and familiar life, close to the people he loved and whose stories and dreams he drew on. That secret wound made me hesitate again as I said goodbye to him: Was this what gave him the courage to carry on the journey despite the uncomfortable conditions?

I was always amazed at how Mahfouz's novels spilled into the streets of Cairo. I remember after I met him in 1989 that I was in a taxi coming from Tahrir Square when we were stopped at the Mosque of Umar by a guy leading a blind man. With them was a young man who had roaming eyes and was wearing a gallabiya. They sat in the back and continued talking among themselves. We understood that the blind man was the imam of the Mosque of Umar and had 'arrested' the young man for stealing its chandelier and was persuading him to return it because it was unlawful to violate the contents of God's house. The blind man and his guide took turns talking and the young man apologized and declared that he would repent for the theft, whatever was required. After they got out the taxi driver started laughing. "What a story, bey. If he stole from the houses of the rich so the mosque could get a chandelier, God would forgive him. But he steals from the house of God. It's mad. People's morals are defunct, no offense. . . ."

I said to myself: This thief does not have the head of Said Mahran, or maybe he is still at the beginning of the road so has surrendered to the influence of Sheikh al-Junaydi. But there is no need for the characters of a novel to conform to reality. What matters is that they themselves become a living reality in people's minds and hearts, in the words of one critic. From this perspective, Mahfouz's characters and spaces create another reality, which is different to ours but which helps us understand it and brings it new life.

At the end of 1996 I was visiting Cairo and went to see the Biennial Exhibition of the Museum of Modern Egyptian Art at the Opera Complex, which included a picture by two Egyptian painters, Adel al-Siwi and someone else whose name I can't remember. I was struck by this picture, which was entitled "Joy without Memory" and consisted of a collage of stones, marble, words, and small drawings. It was large and arresting and led the viewer into a kind of maze, though the "subject" maintained an overwhelming presence. When I returned to the hotel I wrote in my diary: "Is it possible to picture Cairo without the songs of Umm Kulthum, Abd al-Muttalib, and Muhammad Abd al-Wahhab, without Qur'an recitals, the novels of Naguib

Mahfouz, and everything else that embodies the endearing sorrow that lends alleys, dark quarters, and intersecting spaces a special mark? I cannot imagine "Joy without Memory," as the two Egyptian artists propose, not in relation to place or to people. Were it not for the proliferous memory sketched onto places and walls, Cairo could not continue or resist decline by thrusting its radiant memory back so that beautified memories and an embellished past can diminish sadness and allow joy to shine. Yet, man's joy springs from more than memory. Neither the collective imagination and its narratives nor the individual imagination and its fantasies are enough. For there is also the memory woven by the texts of poetry and fiction. Mahfouz's novels are part of the 'added memory' that accompanied my residence in, and visits to, Egypt. This side of memory is special, and happy too, for it does not supplant the existing and ongoing with the repeated and traditional. Rather, whether or not its elements are derived from reality, it is clothed in symbolism and indicates a fantastical memory through which we are able to contemplate things that seem scattered and dispersed or mummified and closed. Joy longs for newness and discovery of the unknown in life. And art does not seek to worship memory and the past but to make it into a living and dynamic realm, nourished by joy, and to bring moments to life. Memory can sometimes be a hindrance, but it is necessary so that fiction does not become a set of images that succeed one another quickly on the smooth surface of the eyes, bereft of the undulations of memory, which recreates images and spaces and connects them to what is buried, ready, in the stores of the collective imagination. What do we understand joy to mean when it pertains to creativity?

Is it not the rare moment in which the artist approaches death in order to scrutinize the world of the living, before weaving 'wedding songs' for them over a memory that draws from a never-ending river?

The Game
of Hallucinations

I DIDN'T STOP VISITING Egypt when I finished studying at the university in 1960. When I recall these visits it seems that most were to do with cultural events, such as seminars and conferences, especially after 1990. So the student of yesterday repaid some of his debt to the Egyptian university and Egyptian culture. Every seminar and meeting was an occasion for enrichment and an opportunity to examine Arab culture and the answers that Egyptian intellectuals and authors were offering to questions that bore an increasingly Arab stamp after the categories of 'center' and 'periphery' began to disappear, opening the way for more essential and complex matters.

The commemoration of Taha Hussein in 1973 at the Arab League was my first opportunity to speak in Cairo as a young critic testing analytical tools derived from a structural method. I was delighted and proud when I greeted my teacher Suhayr al-Qalamawi and heard her words of praise. I remember that a friend accepted my article for the journal *al-Tali'a* and it was published in one of its issues. But my links with the Egyptian cultural scene really began in 1984 at a seminar on modernity organized by the journal *Fusul* and its director, Dr. Izz al-Din Ismail. The climate at the seminar suggested a shift in interest in criticism and thought in Egypt, for *Fusul* conveyed new ideas that were in tune with writings circulating in Lebanon, Tunisia, and Morocco and with questions of creativity and criticism in the global arena at the time. With the large number of Arab critics and intellectuals attending, the seminar seemed to mark the beginning of a new phase for Arab culture in formulating questions relating to society, history, and creativity. The research I presented met with different reactions, but I was happy that this happened in Cairo and that the climate of the discussion promised a resumption on the part of Arab culture of daring projects and suspended questions. During the 1970s there was a sense that Egypt had ceased to play a fundamental role in the development of Arab culture because it was preoccupied with the political struggle and the wave of Sadat's oppression and infitah. I felt that the seminar on modernity reconnected what had been severed and revealed some essential changes in the concerns of Egypt's cultural scene.

Since then I have attended over ten conferences and seminars in Cairo, all of them touching on the problem of culture in its traditional and future dimensions and hovering around defining its new task in the context of withdrawal, the awakening of fundamentalism, the separation of politics from culture, and the division of Arab societies into isolated islands and conflicting spheres. I wonder, as I recall the seminars of the past twenty years and their atmospheres, heated or calm, whether we could use them as a starting point for exploring the place of culture in Egyptian society at this critical time, in which the struggle rages between the culture of enlightenment and openness to modernity and the culture of retreat into the past. I realize that this would not be enough, but I'm convinced that some elements deduced from those seminars and their various debates might be of use in recasting Egyptian culture's relationship with authority, democracy, and civil society.

I reject the attitude of those who, in the name of some obscure revolution, like to blame and vilify Arab intellectuals for selling themselves to regimes and petrodollar institutions and preferring "betrayal" to loyalty to the people. I don't accept it because hundreds of Arab intellectuals and thinkers have been exposed to oppression, arrest, and murder, but their sacrifices have been forgotten. History has not recorded the courage that intellectuals have shown in confronting tyranny with bare chests. I think that some of the shifts in the positions and attitudes of intellectuals require a detailed analysis that would take into account the changes that overtook the cultural sphere and its relationship with politics, authority, and values. Egypt in particular offers a fertile arena for studying the heroic struggle of intellectuals from Abdallah Nadim to Farag Fouda and Nasr Hamid Abu Zayd. But the issue should not be confined to searching for 'heroic' intellectuals. It involves understanding the structure that allowed their emergence and the emergence of others less 'revolutionary,' who, nevertheless, strengthened the fabric of intellectuals and prepared the way for change in a particular context, distinguished by the absence of conditions that in the past permitted the intellectual to be the conscience of the nation, a pioneering thinker, and a guiding philosopher. Egyptian society changed. Its scope widened, life became more complicated, values and manners were shaken, and the political authority that denies civil society a role strengthened. The intellectual had to become a spokesman and follower as opposed to a critic upholding freedom of opinion and rebelling against prevailing ideology. From this perspective, the cultural revolution in Egypt is no longer confined to a few prominent names. Rather, in every sphere of knowledge and social, political, and economic activity, dozens of intellectuals and writers have emerged who rejected totalitarianism and found avenues through which their voices of resistance could be heard. This is an important departure and shouldn't be ignored, for it explains why neither state authority nor regressive extremism were able to erase the presence of the culture of enlightenment and revelatory artistic texts.

In 1992, I was invited to participate in the centenary of the journal *al-Hilal*, "Celebrating a hundred years of enlightenment and modernization." It was a seminar rich in analyses and productive questions for discussion. The subjects centered around the main components of the Nahda in its different phases. In addition to the distinction between the Nahda and the Enlightenment, the relationship with the west, the relative position of the Arab woman, human rights, the role of civil society, democracy, Islam, and the contemporary era were all discussed. Points of view differed at times and concurred at others. When the seminar was over, despite the positive impression I took away from it, a question pressed on me: there had been other seminars treating similar subjects that had produced good analyses, but the missing link that we hadn't yet considered was the way forward now, that is—defining the social and cultural movements capable of continuing Arab activity from where it left off and faltered. Over the decades of revival, Arab movements took action and erupted anew, but at the start of the 1990s, the horizon seemed blocked, nonexistent, for the scene was confined to "marking time" in self-preserving regimes and to acts of violence which exploded out of despair and ignorance in the face of overwhelming impotence. Why had the power of Arab revivalist activity, in its political, cultural, and social transfigurations, disappeared?

This question occupied me and I still cannot claim that there is a clear and convincing answer. Naturally, Arab political and cultural thought produces answers inspired by concepts of civil society and democracy and the accompanying struggle to establish human and civil rights in the Arab world. This is a necessary and decisive goal and would break the siege on the enlightened forces capable of resuming the work of rooting the democratic debate and struggle. But the problem is more complicated than we think, for the liberation of action is dependent on the liberation of discourse and the language of analysis and interpretation. It seems to me that Egyptian culture is currently divided between two discourses: a discourse that mythologizes history and reality—which prevails in most newspapers, media, and religious sermons—and a discourse that preaches modernity and modernization without profoundly or radically criticizing the state, which, in turn, is caught up in protecting itself through violence and opposes the construction of national democratic foundations to bolster dynamic participation in decision-making and protect the inherent rights of the individual.

At the end of February 1993, I was in Cairo to present the translation of my novel *The Game of Forgetting* to an audience at the French Cultural Center. While I was there Ustaz Lutfi al-Khouli got in touch and invited me to take part in an international seminar on thought and creativity, which he was organizing and to which he had invited a selection of thinkers and political analysts, including Regis Dupré, Alain Touraine, Jean Daniel, and Eric Rouleau, as well as a group of Arab writers and intellectuals. I can't judge whether the seminar succeeded in achieving a dialogue between Arab and French thinkers, but lively issues were raised despite differences in opinion at times. I would like to point, in particular, to the contributions of Touraine and Dupré, as they dealt with questions connected with modernity, the communications revolution, and the effects of electronic media.

Touraine spoke about problems of postmodernity in industrial societies. He explained that the original experiment of modernity had ended in failure because technological development and the globalization of economy, media, and culture had led to a schism, which took shape in the domination of consumption based on pragmatism detatched from local identity, which had begun to assert itself in opposition to globalization and clung to cultural, ethnic, and national specificities. Postmodernity was thus associated with a great void produced by the rejection of progress and a disappearance of faith in the historic role of class or nation. Everything fragmented, leaving a huge gap that rendered us vulnerable in the face of violence, prejudice, and racism. All this led to an inability to communicate between people and cultures. In Touraine's opinion, thought in the third millenium must try and find a new structure and reconsider the individual, free from political and religious oppression, striving to realize personal and social freedom, whose material existence bridged the gap between consumer pragmatism, the need for identity, and the practice of giving precedence to daily experience and the self.

Regis Dupré spoke about the huge transformation that societies today had undergone as a result of the endless leaps in information technology. The image, in particular on television, endeavored to present everything close up and as quickly as possible, so that the audience felt as though it was watching events and facts directly and with total transparency. But the issue was more complex than it appeared, for the perceived proximity actually impeded understanding, as it removed the distance that permitted examination and comprehension.

The interruptions and discussions continued in a pleasant, friendly atmosphere and the seminar had the 'international' character that the organizers wanted. On the third day I chaired a session on literature, in which African and European writers and an Egyptian music critic participated. The session proceeded in a normal rhythm then the discussion began. Some of the French participants spoke about the necessity of art's independence from the immediate political and social circumstances. The Egyptian critic next to me on the platform asked to respond to what had been said. I was surprised when he employed a tone different to his usual refined manner of speaking, which matched his elegance and mildness. I can't remember all the details but I recall the first words of his attack: "What culture, what creativity are you talking about, messieurs?" I was seized by laughter and only with great difficulty managed to stifle it. I tried to interrupt and explain to the speaker that there had been a misunderstanding, perhaps because of the instantaneous translation, but he continued to shout and give the foreign visitors a lesson on the relationship between literature and society.

After that seminar and another one organized by the Higher Assembly for Culture in 1997 on "The Future of Arab Culture," I pondered the situation that the Arab intellectual concerned with issues of culture, change, and democracy ought to talk about unrestrainedly, for the past decade had revealed what regimes and analyses had been hiding and covering with make-up and empty discourse. All kinds of violence, blind and savage, had erupted, as though responding to the endless veiled violence practiced by the state under the auspices of made-to-measure laws and constitutions. In most Arab countries violence had flooded the arena, using extremist rhetoric and regressive reinterpretation to impose a mandate that curbed people's movements and ambitions. Gradually a frightening second polarization had appeared: regimes depending on power and authority and domesticated information technology on the one hand, and terrorism breeding in organizations intent on destruction and imposing a regressive guardianship upon citizens on the other. The appearance of this disastrous phenomenon with such force had surprised Arab intellectuals and thinkers and forced them to rethink their relationship with their modern history, with politics and its expressions, and with the social articulation of interpreta-tions rooted in religion, culture, and anthropology. Could we go on writing, analyzing, and striving without defining where the spokesman stood on a map whose roads and borders were lined with bloodstains and signs of mourning?

Many writings and attitudes have been adopted by Arab intellectuals in defense of enlightenment, freedom, and democ-racy, but this was in a context that presumed it was possible to influence regimes to change their power apparatus and support open political movements that cultivate a public mood for demo-cratic change. Then a violent earthquake shook the horizon upon which enlightened Arab intellectuals had been counting. It was no longer possible to write and talk from a position of compro-mise that hoped to "guide" those responsible for the destruction, domestic wars, and cultural disfiguration. Maintaining such a position requires dedication to culture's participation in bringing about a new consciousness to stem the bloodshed.

When I look at the cultural scene in Egypt, I see a clear picture of impeded effectiveness ready to activate collective dynamism and shape issues of "public debate" necessary for the paths and development of nations. I wonder whether the wrongful diminishment of the Egyptian cultural sphere is not the result of its lack of independence from political power. The independence of the cultural scene in Europe and other countries is linked to internal social and political developments that have allowed authors, artists, film directors, dramatists, and intellectuals to establish direct relations with different audiences, and they enjoy relatively good financial situations, which protect them from state control and directives. This evo-lutionary phase was suspended in Egypt in the 1950s, but this should not prevent us from approaching the issue of the cultural sphere's independence from a different perspective that would award its participants the role of taking the initial steps and striving to achieve relative independence from the state. For in Egypt, unlike other Arab societies, there is a great amount and range of intellectual ability and it is playing an increasing role within certain groups of the population, even though it is still bridled and unable to attain the standing that would permit it to undertake criticism and free creativity and to participate in crystallizing a civil society to argue with, and counterbalance, the state. There are hundreds of producers and participants in Egypt's cultural sphere and its effective branches, whether in cinema and drama, universities and institutions, on the radio, or in newspapers, literature, song and music, but still I don't sense any ambition to stop the siege imposed on enlightened Egyptian culture, which as a result cannot enjoy its rightful share of media and forge a direct relationship with the audience. The independence of the cultural sphere is mortgaged on a new contract between intellectuals and the state to organize a democratic struggle in which citizens govern through their reactions, acceptance, and rejection and through the emancipation of art, literature, theater, and cinema from 'controls' exploited for political ends and interests, of which we see examples in the prosecution of the publisher of the *Arabian Nights* and in the censorship of the film *The Emigrant,* and trial of Nasr Hamid Abu Zayd.

The independence of the cultural sphere is not a goal in itself, and achieving it does not ensure better or more effective production, but it is urgently needed in order to stop the suffocation and stumbling, the throng to consumer culture, and the playing on emotions. There is an aspiration these days for a bold, critical culture that would talk about the unsaid, repose suppressed questions, and enter the suggestive worlds of fiction. People are no longer carried away by slogans and promises and ready-made ideological solutions. They live in the phase of 'decline' with eyes wide open, searching for cultural spaces to dissipate the illusion, construct a liberated consciousness amid the ruins of setbacks, and offer the individual a horizon.

On a recent visit, I was talking to an Egyptian writer friend and the conversation led to the Egyptian and Arab cultural situation, the 'resignation' and contradictions we perceived in attitudes and positions, and the disappearance of culture's influence on politics. He told me that several intellectuals were saying the same things we were and that hundreds of journalists had written about these thorny and interconnected topics, but he didn't think Egypt's intellectuals were capable any longer of effecting a change in consciousness or bringing about a reality that strove to transcend the stagnation, rigidity, and wooden language. When I asked him his reasons, he replied that the state's structures were too strong and, although it expended a lot on culture, its cultural policy did not proceed fluently or decisively toward enlightenment and free creativity. This ultimately produced a dubious balance that was tipped in favor of the producers of lowbrow culture and propaganda. All intellectuals could benefit from the state's cultural apparatus, but disparities, favoritism, and the political balance led to a marginalization of intellectuals and artists whose names were connected with modern Egyptian culture.

As I listened to my friend I remembered two texts that differed in both form and language and were written a long time apart. One was by the short story writer and novelist Yusuf Idris (at the end of the 1970s), entitled "The Game," and the other was by a friend, the critic Gaber Asfour, entitled "Hallucinations" and published at the beginning of 1997. These two texts came together in their successful representation of the situation of the Egyptian (and Arab) intellectual through a literary metaphor, rich in suggestion and imagery, depicting the intellectual's relationship with all-embracing institutions and the dynamics of power. I found that the story "The Game," with its subtle description and Kafkaesque atmosphere, and the free text "Hallucinations," with its poetic language and nightmarish dream images, closely represented the situation of the Arab intellectual, which often resembled Sisyphus' ordeal, or worse, for the Arab intellectual pushed a rock on a vast, endless expanse and could barely see a peak or place to aim for.

In "The Game" the writer describes the experience of a newcomer to a smart, elegant gathering where he feels like a stranger. Nevertheless, he wants to have a go at the game that is shown to him by a man carrying a box filled with bullets, including one that looks different to the others, with a black gun in his right hand.

"Do you want to have a go, sir?"

The newcomer pays to take part in the game. He wants to use the different-looking shiny bullet but the game-master deals underhandedly to prevent him from having it and the other guests assist in the procrastination and deception. The newcomer dives on the man, grabs him by the front of his jacket, and punches and hits him, but the game-master submits and continues to smile impudently. When he is exhausted he stops the beating but the game-master carries on smiling and offering the gun and bullets, the unusual metal one still not in its place. There is nothing left for the newcomer, having used up all his strength, but to seek refuge in accusations and blame, to which the game-master replies, "Didn't I say, do you want to have a go, sir? You just have." Then adds, "This *is* the game."

In my interpretation of "The Game"—which was not the only one—I saw the newcomer to the party as a symbol of the intellectual who is excluded from the tents of power in a game that soaks up his effort, integrity, and talent and turns him into froth that rises to the surface then disappears. The rules of the game are clear and harsh, and designed to prevent him from using the effective bullet and force him to use debased weapons that can't change the existing order in any way.

In "Hallucinations," which uses the first-person narrator, the dream-story centers on a man who finds himself in a gathering of people with whom he has no connection or common language: "I was overcome by an oppressive feeling that I didn't belong here, that I was somewhere I shouldn't be, seeing things I didn't want to see and hearing things I didn't want to hear. . . ." The narrator's nightmarish journey carries on, lined with specters and characters from the *Arabian Nights* and *Kalila wa Dimna*, until he comes to a wide hall with chairs arranged in a semicircle before a huge, awesome throne. The people sitting there are dressed in different sorts of cloaks and hoods, embellished with "a new kind of power that my feet lead me to." No one takes any notice of him and he feels like a stranger but, at the same time, he is drawn toward what seems to be a modern-day emperor, though everything inside him wants to get out of there. He is overcome with feelings of ennui and alienation but decides to gather his breath before resuming the journey in search of somewhere that will heed him and to which he can belong and avoid succumbing to the hallucinations that seem to hover around him like flies on his frightening dream-journey.

From the perspective of an interpretation in which the narrator symbolizes the intellectual, the text of "Hallucinations" reveals the futile relationship imposed on the intellectual by authority to turn him into a merely decorative element, a mere fly whose hum no one pays any attention to within tents of authority draped in technological power and expressions of luxury.

For over thirty years the dysfunctional relationship between intellectuals and authority has prevented culture from undertaking criticism, shaping fundamental questions, and invigorating dynamic change. The "game of hallucinations" represents a fixed stance adopted by the state that encapsulates the fundamental and perennial incompatibility between culture, as a reflection of the history of society and its profound mutations, and power that strives to assimilate and reproduce compliant values and censored relations as a means of control.

On the contemporary Egyptian scene literary, creativity destabilizes the "game of hallucinations" through texts that refuse to echo prevailing ideological discourses or defend a ready-made value system. Since the 1980s, texts have been published that differ from their predecessors insofar as their authors don't want to appear to support an ideology, institution, or party. From among the ruins, feelings of bitterness and marginalization, works by young Egyptian writers have emerged which draw inspiration from the deep cracks and increasing division between the state's desire to modernize from above and the marginalized, oppressed, and skeptical majority, who listen to their inner voice searching for its own language and questions. I think that this incongruence between the representation of the individual and the group, which is embodied in the difference between literary texts and official or sacred cultural discourse, makes artistic creativity a means for understanding what is happening beneath the surface, fluctuating between light and darkness, and, perhaps, paving the way for the necessary recognition of the cultural sphere's autonomy and for the shattering of the game of hallucinations.

During the summer of 1995, I was invited to an evening gathering of a widow and her three grownup sons. After supper they suggested that they show the guests some silent short films, which their deceased father had made in the 1950s when the family lived in Cairo. The films depicted the mother, the children when they were young, and some relatives, most of whom I knew. Forty years had passed since the images in these silent films and we were able to see the gradual phases of the family's lives over a period of between five and ten years. As we watched that evening, we could study the difference between the people gathered around the screen and the same people in their childhood and youth forty years ago.

Raw Narrative
Walks on Two Feet

DURING THE SHOWING, DESPITE a stream of humorous remarks, compensating for the films' silence, I was glued to the powerful metaphor emitted by the silent images, which condensed a large portion of the life of each person depicted in swift movements, words they spoke but could no longer remember, places they inhabited and visited, and loved ones and friends who had died or from whom they had been separated. No doubt watching themselves that evening brought some of them pleasure or stirred regrets. But I did not think that a spectacle of this kind would match the intimacy that is produced by a retreat into memory to retrieve scenes from your life or probe dense moments with the joy and sorrow they contain. Why was writing, in one of its fundamentals, a dialogue with memory and the creation of a kind of 'film production' for it, and so made our lives longer and more enduring than the silent images were able to? I wondered.

I don't stand by this analysis of writing anymore, however. For it doesn't take into account what happens when memory's contents are entered into a wider context, namely the romanesque, with its diverse and ambiguous interpretations. On one level the romanesque refers to the raw material that creates the sequence of events, while on another level it means something else when related to that which breaks the ready-madeness and monotony of things. On the level of writing, it is the principal thematic features upon which textual elements are built. Thus the word romanesque has several meanings. Nevertheless, as far as I can see, it preserves common features whether it derives from the real world, films and television, or reading. So it is difficult to compare the image and the word, whose influence in both instances has to do with something that transcends the means of expression.

When I recall the romanesque that my memory accumulated from Egypt, I cannot place boundaries between what I read, saw in reality or on screen, or heard in tales. I think all these, collectively, weave a phantasmagoria that is essential to some of the relationships between means of expression and Egypt's spaces in their concrete form.

Is it, then, enough for me to recall some of the romanesque that my memory accumulated from real-life scenes? Or would it be more in keeping with my imagination and memory to also follow the stream of cinematic images in the Egyptian films that I watched, which 'created' fictional worlds directly and mixed them with the reality I was gradually discovering, adding to it new romanesque dimensions?

I cannot here recount every film whose features have taken root in my memory, for such a project would require a special effort and should probably be executed collectively so that cinema's treasures are not lost to those writings that endeavor to recover ever-elusive "reality." It is enough here to point out a

few moments of Egyptian cinema that accompanied the forma-
tion of my image-memory and its store of romanesque.

The first films I watched as a child in Fez left a velvety impression on me and my memory, for they were shored up with singing (Muhammad Abd al-Wahhab, Farid al-Atrash, Asmahan,
Umm Kulthum) and with décor, clothes, and sets that imitated
luxurious European houses. Thus as I watched *The White Rose*,
Long Live Love, *Love and Revenge*, and *The Pasha's Daughter*,
I entered a rosy romantic world adorned with songs, evening
soirées, women's laughter, and beautiful girls in fashionable
dresses. The love stories and the tears that sometimes pervaded
them told of the promised paradise awaiting me when I entered
young adulthood.

When I arrived in Cairo in the mid-1950s, I began watching
films that were inspired by real life and moved a little away from
the velvety shell to allow the camera to enter the spaces of ordinary people in towns and in the countryside *(Good Day Sinner,
Raya and Sakina, A Woman's Young Man, Bab al-Hadid)*. There
were also the funny and refreshing comedies, especially those in
which the hero was played by famous actors like Naguib al-Rihani,
Ismail Yasin, Abd al-Salam al-Nabulsi, and Abd al-Munim Ibrahim. A medley of characters, spaces, and languages drawn from
Egypt's romanesque in a restless vision that alternated between
popularism and entertainment adapted to public tastes.

Now, as I think back to my relationship with the Egyptian
cinema, I recall an article published by Yusuf Idris in a newspaper at the end of the 1950s entitled "Shadiism" after the actress
and singer Shadya. I can't find the article now, but I remember that the writer tried to present Shadiism as a code of life
that manifested in the conduct and sentiments of certain city-
dwellers who imitated Shadiya and adopted her as a symbol
of desirable pampering, sentimentality, and bourgeois living,
supported by an imaginary balance of values. It was a good

'snapshot' and Yusuf Idris shaped it with his irony and penetrating language to bring out a variety of the contradictions of Nasserism, divided as it was between socialist intentions and actually enjoying life.

It seems to me now that Shadiism, with its ambiguity, repressed eroticism, and tearful songs, compensated for the sexual and emotional freedom denied by social conventions and tradition. Recently I re-watched *My Wife's Devil* by the director Faten Abd al-Wahhab, in which Shadiya plays the title role with Salah Zulfiqar and Adel Imam. The idea guiding the film is the influence of foreign films on the wife's imagination. When she returns home, influenced by what she has seen at the cinema, she becomes a different woman, released from the ties that bind her, and obsessed by film scenes, which she begins to apply in the house, thereby shattering her life's monotonous rhythm and rebelling against repressive social attitudes. The wife (Shadiya) flirts openly with one of her husband's friends at an evening gathering, imitating what she saw in *Irma La Douce*. Another day she imagines her husband as Tarzan or an unvanquished fighting hero with her beside him, applauding his brilliant victories. In one of these imaginary, compensatory scenes, the wife says to her husband, "I want our life to be full of emotion. I want people to talk about you and I'll say (she sings):

| Oh love of mine | My knight in shining armor. |
| Oh love of my heart | Oh love of my life." |

We find similar scenes repeated in different ways by actresses like Iman, Lubna Abd al-Aziz, Magda, and others belonging to the family of Shadiism in its broad sense.

I think it is possible to distinguish between two different moments in Egyptian cinema, which can be called "Shadiism" and "Chahinism" (after the director Youssef Chahine).

In the first moment, as Nasserism took root, Shadiism emerged in songs (Abd al-Halim Hafez, Fayza Ahmad, and others) and films (a group of Ihsan Abd al-Quddous and Yusuf al-Siba'i's novels adapted for the screen) and expressed a longing for individuality, for which the spread of university education among the lower and middle classes, alongside a re-estimation of the peasant and poor on the level of legislation, paved the way. All this increased the value of the individual and opened the way for him to express his true self. However though films inspired by the new political values appeared, the inherent limitations of Egyptian cinema from the time of Talaat Harb and his industrial project, with all its social ramifications, continued to influence public taste and the way that society, which itself evolved under the influence of cinema, was represented. It was from this fundamental function that Shadiism derived its power and legitimacy in a political system that professed a different ideology.

Chahinism, on the other hand, only appeared in some of Youssef Chahine's later films, after the end of Nasserism. By Chahinism, I mean the opening of the way for film scripts to bring to the fore the individual who confronts questions and struggles imposed by society and its institutions. I am thinking in particular of two films, *Alexandria . . . Why?* and *Alexandria Again and Forever*, for they shifted Egyptian film away from recording reality and methods of constructing it toward accentuating the self and its intimate components and fantasies. However, this tendency was limited and is lacking even in Chahine's recent films. Thus Egyptian cinema, despite some innovation in technique and production, seems to be marking time for it clings to binarism (good/evil, authentic values/false values), and this determines its thematic worlds and methods of cinematic narrative.

Sometimes, when contemplating events and findings that I came across living or visiting Egypt, I say to myself: If I'd had a camera and recorded them directly, I'd now have unique fragments of romanesque that could break the mold of Egyptian films with their set idioms and ready-made expressions.

At the end of the 1980s, I was visiting Cairo and the Spanish writer Juan Goytisolo was in town. We agreed to meet at three in the afternoon in the cafeteria at the Cosmopolitan Hotel. We ordered tea and plunged into a conversation about his visit to Egypt and the scripts he had written for Spanish television. There was no one else apart from us in the cafeteria, but at one point a tall, large blind man entered, led by a young boy and girl, neither of whom could have been older than nine. The blind man asked the girl to describe the room and its contents and whether there were other customers. Then he asked the boy to slip his hand up his back, under his shirt and woolen pullover, and scratch it for him. The boy untucked his shirt from under his belt and put his hand inside and reached up, standing on tiptoe to reach the itch, while the blind man leaned forward a little so that the boy's fingers could get closer. Juan and I watched the scene, smiling, and when the scratching exercise was over the small procession turned and left in silence, just as it had entered, as though we hadn't been there.

Two years ago I arrived in Cairo at five in the morning. When I came out of the airport's outer hall I was surrounded by taxi and coach drivers offering their services and competing among themselves to win customers. A burly young man warded them off and offered me a suitable price so I agreed to put an end to the shouting battle. The young man owned a large Honda and had two youths with him to help out. On the way to the hotel he began apologizing for the onslaught that I'd received from the taxi drivers and talking about his difficult circumstances and bad luck: "My father, God bless him, was a boxing hero so I wrestle taxi drivers. If only he'd made a soccer player out of me, I'd be rich and well off. Better off than I am now."

On the same visit I took a taxi that already had a customer, or friend of the driver, inside. I sat in the backseat and followed their conversation. Baldness was attacking the driver's head, disguising his youth. His face had grown dark and his features seemed to have lost their light. His conversation was calm and exuded a sad irony. He said to the man sitting beside him as we passed close to the Nile Sheraton, "If you sold this car you could spend two nights in the Sheraton. How superb. It's clean. You'd eat good food, dance, stay up till morning, and forget about the squalor I live in." He was silent for a bit then went on, "But you can do these things for less. I'd get a maid to clean the flat and cook me chicken, lamb, and baked macaroni and buy a bottle of whisky to cheer me up. I'd be as happy as could be . . . right?"

In a café frequented by intellectuals and writers, I listened to the following conversation:

"Did you read that female television presenters are being forbidden from wearing tight trousers?"

"Why? Isn't it a good thing? I mean it helps clear communication."

"Clear indeed! Are you kidding. Shouldn't you pay attention to positive decisions instead of carrying on your silly criticism?"

"I'm not joking or criticizing. I'm being literal. I think modern women should have the right to wear tight trousers as they can use them to catch the attention of the inadvertent."

"Nobody's inadvertent these days. Men's eyes are telescopes. They see what's visible and hidden, and what's beneath the skin."

"So why should they deprive us of tight trousers on television then?"

◉

I always wonder why the image of the woman I saw at the Mosque of Sinan Pasha comes to me from time to time. I was walking through the quarter of Bulaq Abul Ela on my way to visit the Mosque of Sinan Pasha, which I had heard much about. I entered the porticos and wandered about the mosque's expanses, then stopped in the space behind the fountain. There my eyes fell on a large woman whose body was almost square. She was wearing a tattered shirt, which was torn at the edges, and had a red bow on her forehead. She was lying on her back, wallowing on the tiles of the courtyard at the back of the mosque, as though intoxicated by the rays of the April sun. There was a smile on her lips and her eyes were half open but not looking at anything in particular. There was no else around and she wasn't aware of me. I didn't stand there long so as not to disturb her rapture in that wonderful retreat. I still remember the face of the woman, intoxicated and alone in the courtyard of the Mosque of Sinan Pasha, wallowing on the tiles and stroking her body with her hands like a cat in heat.

◎

Cairo's romanesque, for me, is specifically linked to the spoken language—meaningful and meaningless, as they say—that bursts forth from taxi drivers, pedestrians conversing in streets and cafés, friends chatting, telephone conversations, talk on the radio, television, and in the theater, and from the newspapers.

On a recent visit I telephoned an Egyptian friend. We talked a little while about health, affairs in Morocco, and literature, then the conversation took the following turn: "Say, come and sit with me a little and we can chat. I'll make you a cup of tea to cheer you up and tell you about the dancer whom they're detaining in the Gulf because her passport has run out and the consulate is on holiday. Goodness! Her husband is protesting but no one is listening. According to *al-Akhbar*, they're saying that they appointed her to teach Egyptian dance to girls in the Gulf. It's a rumor and everyone's talking about it. Apparently she is thriving in her teaching job and money is being lavished on her like rice. But her husband is crying on the television every day. He's jealous as she used to dance here in his nightclub. Listen, he used to stand guard over her, but now she's miles away from him and the devil is everywhere. He doesn't know what she is up to. He has twenty days of mental torture before the consulate reopens. What do you reckon? Should the ministry of culture intervene and return the dancer to her husband? No. It would be censorship of art. Plus the ministry doesn't know if the passport has actually run out or if the dancer is just using it as a ruse so she can perform her art freely. Hey! We have good artistic freedom, don't we?"

I see reading the Egyptian newspapers as part of bathing in the romanesque out of which news, anecdotes, tales, and battles that don't end except to begin again are woven. It is difficult to imagine the wheels of government and the population turning or Egypt's public affairs continuing without the newspapers. Television and radio play an important role, but newspapers are popular because of their relative freedom in criticizing and exposing, which is lacking in visual and audio media. People's attachment to the newspapers, it seems to me, has to do with its history of drafting news, writing controversial articles, and keeping abreast of the secrets of artists, important men, and politicians, which creates a kind of balance between the few who monopolize political action and decision-making and enjoy great revolutions and the majority who take pleasure in following news of scandals, stars' performances, and the struggles of the political elite. Most Egyptian newspapers attempt to thrill and excite and include novel subjects. Two examples will suffice here. One is a battle between the Sunni and Shi'a, the other is the kidnap of a fourteen-year-old girl:

Rose al-Yusuf reported, "A case about the propagation of Shi'i ideas has never been presented to the court before, despite the arrest of people like the accused." What is interesting here is that the battle flared up and the battleground moved from the religious newspaper *al-Liwa' al-islami* to *al-Haqiqa* and *Rose al-Yusuf*. The inevitable result was Sunni attacks on Shi'a. In its Saturday issue, *al-Haqiqa* published the details of the judicial inquiry and some commentary, foremost among which was an account of Shaykh Hasan's recorded sermons. It reported, "Shaykh Hasan Shahata began his seminar on Muhammad's descendents saying, 'The Prophet came to al-Sayyida Fatima al-Zahraa one day and she said to him, "Oh father, your face is lit up today." He said, "How can my face not be lit up when Gabriel has come to me and told me that God has created seven souls among us, which he did not create among our forefathers and others like them." She said, "Who are they, Prophet of God?" He said, "You, your husband and your children, and among us, Hamza the master of witnesses, Jaafar al-Tayyar, who flies with the angels, and al-Mahdi, who fills the earth with justice."' Shaykh Hasan reviews the hadith, whose soundness is not known, saying, 'No one in the world is honored except through membership of the House of the Prophet. People of commendation and honor are proud to extol the House of the Prophet. People say God help Sayyid Hussein. But do they say God help Abu Bakr or Umar? Everyone would laugh. They would say it is irrational. Nor God help Uthman, Uthman the doorman. Every doorman is called Uthman. Uthman the cursed, the first to steal from the Muslim treasury. The ignorant say he was the one with two lights. Who had two lights? Imam Ali, because of Hasan and Hussein. Our Lord's grace is extensive. Every doorman is called Uthman!'"

The second example is an event that seems to have actually occurred, according to *al-Gomhuria*. Two Egyptian workers kidnapped a fourteen-year-old schoolgirl and kept her in their room where they contented themselves with examining her naked body without touching her. The newspaper said that "the young girl was on her way to visit her relatives in al-Haram, south-west of Cairo, when three young men surrounded her and tried to drag her away with them. She shouted for help and the two workers, who were also on the road, intervened, fought the three young men, and were able to get them off her. The two workers escorted the young woman to their room so she could wash her face and drink some water. However, they drugged her drink and she woke up the next morning and found herself naked. The two workers denied assaulting her, insisting they only wanted to look at her naked body. The public prosecutor sentenced them to four days in prison while they helped with the police inquiry."

On a recent visit to Cairo (February 1998), I noticed the newspapers' interest in 'baltaga,' or thuggery. After reading a few reports I realized that Shadiism had furrowed under the toes of criminals, who used acid to disfigure their victims' faces, and under the punches of baltaga thugs who were addicted to bango, snorting substances, and shooting drugs. What was strange was the consensus that the 'flourishing' of baltaga at this moment in time was to do with a broad collaboration of school pupils, male and female, who were injecting themselves in lavatories and selling bango in schools. Who would believe it? Yet it was simply another aspect of the dark romanesque that attacks Arab and foreign societies alike. Nevertheless, I commended the Egyptian press for turning the phenomenon into a subject for general discussion, participated in by fathers, mothers, and educators as well as the minister of education, who, besides other reasons for the spread of baltaga, mentioned the "checkbook dad," who was absent from the family, abroad, and often made do, together with his wife, with sending checks to his sons and daughters. On the level of officials, baltaga took on more dangerous dimensions because it began to challenge the laws of state and confront the security forces with violence. The baltaga thugs stole, raped, abducted, and imposed taxes on merchants and the wealthy, leading some journalists to point to the similarity between the baltaga and the futuwwa, who were widespread in city quarters and popular alleys for a long time and who provided Naguib Mahfouz with many characters in his stories and novels. However, the baltaga and the futuwwa were very different, for the latter intervened to help the weak and see that they got their right in the face of the shameless rich. Several waters had flowed since the time of *Palace Walk*, Nasserism, and "Shadiism." Baltaga in its current state was like a torrential stream against which neither pacifying words nor new legislation were of any use.

I remember that four years ago I wrote a short piece entitled "Cairo Lost in the Mist of Clamor and Violence." Some Egyptian friends read it and weren't impressed by my emphasis on the role of the spoken language in spreading a type of false communication, vital to institutions, daily comforts and people caught in the net of "decline." On a trip to Alexandria with Edwar al-Kharrat and Said al-Kafrawi, the discussion led to the contents of that piece and I found that they disagreed with the pessimistic tone that shimmered through my words, for Egypt possessed an historical and spiritual depth which was not visible but worked in secret to resurrect tombs and restore the hope latent in hearts that appeared defeated and humiliated. I did not share this "faith" that brought miracles in bygone times, for a lot had changed in the world and in people, who did not know how to confront an open sewer that destroyed the emotional elements that used to push men to rebel and revolt from time to time. How could we continue to count on them in a national context (from water and desert to water and desert) that ground down the citizen's spirit and erased everything that made the Arab a human with freedom and will?

When I wrote that piece I was not trying to "see what I wanted." Rather, I was suffering under the weight of surveillance, feelings of despair, and a bitterness that could not be cured with the pretext of a return of the hidden spirit. Texts are entitled to be aggressive to what or whom they wish, and reality, with all its surprises, is entitled to disprove our angry meditations.

During the same visit in 1995, an artist friend, Badr al-Deeb, invited me to lunch with some friends. The conversation led to what I had written about Cairo and he made an astute and suggestive observation. As I recall, he said to me, "I agree with you that Egyptians talk a lot, but it's to hide the eerie silence deep inside them. Silence is death for them so they raise their voices with talk."

It is impossible to imagine a romanesque without the existence of language. This is a platitude that requires no corroboration. Levels and dimensions of language differ, and it is often just chatter. When I recall my relationship with the romanesque stored in my memory, it seems entangled and intermeshed, for I cannot retrieve "my own language" except through the language of Egypt's romanesque. In the beginning I was captivated by this new Arabic tongue that my childhood memory picked up from songs and films and then living in Cairo. Gradually my own language became hidden in the folds of my memory, as I used the language of the present, which was infatuated with political action and the construction of a different society. It was as though the frenzy of the future eliminated the past and the language stored in my memory. For twenty years I proceeded as though blindfolded. I stumbled constantly and increasingly felt that I was going round in an empty circle. On a visit to Cairo at the end of the 1970s, I experienced a kind of awakening of the language buried in my body and memory. I began to perceive that other parallel world, which was woven by the language of Egypt's romanesque and which short story writers and novelists drew inspiration from to construct charming and attractive worlds. I began to ask myself whether Morocco's romanesque was not mute in comparison to its Egyptian counterpart, or whether my captivation at the end of adolescence was what made me think so.

The veil began to lift from my eyes. I had spent my childhood in Fez in a large house in an old quarter, a milieu of everyday language, ritual, and religious ceremonies. That language, which I had stored away and ignored, was not woven from a void but linked to a romanesque with its own peculiarity and distinctive features. Was my forgetfulness part of an attempt to protect that 'unknown' side of myself which I used to think shaped me? Why was I intent on ignoring a childhood brimming with language, dreams, and mischief? I had written pages and a number of beginnings for a journey of discovery that visited the worlds of childhood, but they were left hanging and unfinished. Perhaps I was afraid that writing would absorb me in nostalgia for the past and its magic. When I began to comprehend the power of the romanesque and its language's transcendence of temporal categories, as though it was a refuge against the extinction of things and people, I abandoned myself to writing *The Game of Forgetting* in a quest for a romanesque recreated by an adventure of words and rescued from the past's embrace so that windows and apertures looking onto concerns of the present and aspirations of the future could be opened before it.

Yet I don't think that writing entirely corresponds to a particular romanesque. It always has the power to escape the clasp of the lines and marks on the page to dwell in its own anarchic system, which is why the text derives its value, first and foremost, from its existence within non-homogenous concord and harmonious strangeness. Moreover, it is open to what is stored in the reader's imagination.

Another challenge confronts me as I contemplate the question of romanesque: can we exchange extravagant verbal expression for a more economical one? If we feel the presence and existence of the romanesque in all that we read or hear, why do we depend so much on language and words to evoke it? For example, I have in mind two novels by Gabriel García Márquez: *One Hundred Years of Solitude*, which he wrote with linguistic and verbal abundance, and *Chronicle of a Death Foretold*, which he wrote with excessive economy, sticking closely to the romanesque and barely departing from it. A subtler example is found in Samuel Beckett's work, which uses language and words that depend on silence, as though insisting that relations between things, beings, and mankind are too intricate and delicate for language to penetrate: the reader must be reminded of the silence that words leave behind in our souls in order to make way for that which is understood through means other than language.

On my last visit to Cairo, a writer friend telephoned me one night and said, "Hey, let's write a novel together. We'll base it on your 'narrative walks on two feet' idea. Hey, listen. I know a story, I'll summarize its general idea for you. It's a true story and will amaze you. A guy called Abd al-Muhsin lived in Imbaba but one day he had enough. His wife hassled him all the time and his children were growing up and their demands were increasing. He had many debts that he couldn't pay and the shop wasn't enough, so he decided to have himself declared officially dead. He announced it in *al-Ahram* but in the statement reserved the right to resume life in another quarter, which the paper didn't mention but I know was Shubra. There he began a new life with curiosities that will amaze you and amaze the reader. Look, I know his address. We could write the novel and then go and interview him and add the interview to the text. It would be an unusual thing to do. Isn't this the kind of romanesque you're looking for?"

After that conversation I began thinking about a novel based on a counter-romanesque that used language sparingly and did not surrender to the magic of words. Through the labyrinths of my imagination the features of a romanesque emerged that lent itself to an economic form that had not hitherto seemed achievable. I decided to call this narrative, "The Walker." Its protagonist is an employee on the railways, aged over fifty, with a beautiful wife who understands his temperament and habits. He has two sons, who have grown up and left home, and he lives a wholesome life with his wife and a friend's family, with whom they exchange visits. He waits patiently for retirement so that he and his wife can travel to parts of North Africa that he hasn't seen, but his wife suddenly has a heart attack and the doctors are unable to do anything to save her life. The man cuts himself off for long weeks then decides to give up work and devote himself to walking the streets of Rabat until late at night. He finds nothing that interests him so he remains attached to the specter of his deceased wife and goes on watching the world around him on his wanderings. One night, three adolescents dressed in American shirts and trousers, wearing helmets that are older than they are on their heads, block his path. They threaten him and demand he gives them all the money on him. He complies pleasantly and apologizes for only having a few dirhams but promises to give them a reasonable amount the following day. This is the beginning of the man's friendship with the errant adolescents. He spends his days walking around and watching people and cars, and in the evening he meets them at the entrance to one of the public gardens to listen as they relate their thieving adventures that day. Their language is spare and their words concise. As the days pass he begins to believe he is changing into an adolescent fugitive like them and that he is living through them. Every evening, when they tell him about their adventures in concise words, a world opens up in his imagination, expanding and multiplying, especially when he returns home and lies on his bed, trying to sleep. In the morning he returns to walking the streets of Rabat: the man walks with the romanesque beside him, on two feet.

A Pharaoh in
a Cotton Shroud

AT THE END OF November in 1996 my feet led me to the Cairo Museum one morning so that I could recover specters of the grand statues, mummies, vessels, and sarcophagi.

This time the desire to visit the museum came after reading about the journey of Ramesses II's mummy around the burial grounds of Thebes, Deir al-Bahari, and Paris before finally coming to rest in one of the large halls of Cairo Museum. For three thousand years the embalmed body of Ramesses II had remained present in life in death, perhaps hoping to be resurrected to resume life in the kingdoms of eternity. But, unlike other pharaohs, he would not remain prostrate in his sarcophagus, surrounded by gold and silver objects and papyri full of prayers and funerary texts, anticipating the resurrection that would restore him to eternal life in accordance with the teachings of priests and promises of deities. Rather he came out, shrouded, to look down on the lives of ordinary people. The first time his rich burial ground was exposed to several instances of plundering at the hands of the inhabitants of Thebes was between 1080 and 1150 BC. The twenty-first dynasty of priests were not able to save the goods and precious objects that eased the pharaoh's loneliness, so they saved what they considered to be essential: the body of Ramesses II and the bodies of other pharaohs connected to the new state. A priest oversaw the repair of Ramesses' mummy, surrounded it with lilies and lotus blossoms, and prayed that it would arrive safely on the shores of eternity, which awaited the newly buried in Deir al-Bahari. Almost three thousand years later, in 1881, an Egyptian peasant discovered a cellar full of the mummies of great pharaohs in Deir al-Bahari, foremost among them Ramesses II, whom the French scholar Gaston Maspero identified and wrote about: "He looks like he is dozing, immersed in a peaceful sleep. . . . Can we picture this thin, slender body breathing with life so long ago when we look at it now? His features survive. The subject looks virginal to the extent that we waver between dazzlement and anxiety." And indeed it was anxiety that I felt as I examined the mummy of Ramesses II that morning in the cedar sarcophagus, wrapped in a cotton shroud.

Although he lived for over ninety years in his first life, his small thin face, with its delicate features, looked like that of an infant child. His hands were clasped on his chest and his sleeping body was wrapped in a white cotton sheet in the middle of an open sarcophagus, which was stripped of its original gold embellishment and tokens of royalty and majesty. Perhaps it was this nakedness that made me feel like I was before a fetus fresh from the womb. I was suddenly overcome by anxiety, for his face and childlike characteristics reminded me of the unnamed child I buried over twenty years earlier, a baby who inhaled the breezes of life for half an hour and whose bare face, closed eyes, and blind movements only enjoyed a few moments but planted its image firmly in my mind. I was confused and

156

silent as I carried it to the cemetery by the sea. "It's what God ordained, friend. God bless you," my friend comforted me. Now, in the museum, I trembled violently before the embalmed body of Ramesses II, who pursued 'life' in death, challenging the laws of extinction. The melancholy I felt, it seemed to me, was not warranted, for my bonds with the newborn child left a wound that I had got used to and registered under the column of forgetting, while the mummy of Ramesses swept me into lands of being and non-being and continued life. If Ramesses had remained in his original sarcophagus, wearing his 'mask' and surrounded by pearls, jewelry, statues, and gold vessels, I would not have felt that he had that same fragility that renders us a drop in a sand dune or speck swirling about in a tornado's vortexes. But, half-naked with his childlike face and hidden smile, he forced his presence on us and asked us about things we usually pass over in silence. Ramesses II ruled for nearly sixty-seven years, married at least five times, had beautiful concubines, fathered over a hundred sons and daughters, erected cities, huge statues, the temple of Abu Simbel in south Egypt, six rock temples in Nubia, and plunged into successive wars to secure his empire, while poets recorded fierce battles to perpetuate the memory of his victory in Kadesh. When he died he was over ninety years old.

This pharaoh, whose likenesses and exploits filled the land of Egypt for over three thousand years, was not content with what he had prepared for entering the world of eternity, as he and his ancestors believed they would. So after his tomb was pilfered and plundered in the Valley of the Kings and his mummy was transported to Deir al-Bahari, archaeologists brought him into the life of museums to discover, in the seventh decade of the twentieth century, that a fungal disease had begun to gnaw his bones and was threatening his embalmed corpse. The effectiveness of the embalming was running out and the deceased Ramesses was dying a final death, which would prevent his soul restoring his body to live, in another world, a life similar to the one he lived on earth. All ancient Egypt's fans sounded the alarm bells to save Ramesses' ailing corpse and, on September 26, 1976, the great emperor's mummy left the Cairo Museum on the back of a truck, heading for the airport. Before Cairo came to life, a French archaeologist, Christiane Desroches Noblecourt, asked the captain of the airplane to circle the Pyramids so that, 3,190 years after his death, Ramesses II could look down on one of the Seven Wonders of the World. When the plane arrived at the airport in Paris, Ramesses found an official reception worthy of his majesty. Then he was moved to a special hall in the Museum of the People, near the Eiffel Tower, where over a hundred scholars and doctors set about his treatment, devoting themselves to analyzing particular bones in order to identify a type of parasite with the wonderful name Daedalea biennis, and staying up long nights until they discovered the right kind of healing rays. Meetings were convened between specialists in order to avoid results that might disfigure Ramesses' cells and tissues or cause his remaining hair to fall out. The French scholars rejoiced at their success in restoring the whole body to its soul roaming the skies of eternity. But Ramesses was the greatest victor, for he resisted a fate worse than death: erosion, oblivion, and the extinction of the dream-body.

It's as though Ramesses II is saying to us, "Make a dream from your body and a body from your dream," I muttered to myself at the end of my visit. When I cast a final look at him, I thought that his face fitted Maspero's account well: "A sweet and peaceful smile still hovers on his lips and his half-closed eyelids emit a kind of light from beneath the lashes, which were once moist and lustrous. The light comes from the reflection of the white porcelain eyes, which were placed in the sockets at the time of embalming."

Ancient Egyptian civilization abounds with statues and depictions of gods who tuned the rhythm of life on the banks of the Nile and furnished the spaces of legends that gathered up the human and real and shaped them in sacred utterances and rituals. Nearly two thousand gods filled the imagination, existence, and vision of the ancient Egyptians, and the majority of them were affiliated to the animal kingdom: the falcon, the swift, the heron, the frog, the eel, the locust, the scarab, the ox . . . they even had bad omens among these deities, such as the scorpion. In the beginning, they selected animals as symbols to represent their gods, thus the god Khnum was a goat, Horus was a falcon, Thoth was the ibis, and Sobek was a crocodile. Then, at a later stage, the gods began to take on human form and borrow human semblances, so we find them portrayed in temples and paintings with human heads and limbs and, indeed, wearing Egyptian clothing. Even the animal deities took on human shapes, thus Sishus appears as a man with a crocodile's head and Horus has the head of a falcon, and they put two horns to symbolize a cow on the head of the goddess Hathor. In another stage the gods would wear human faces and have special places of worship designated to them, after they had begun moving around in nature, far away from rituals. At this stage symbols were introduced to organize the relationship between the universe, elements of nature, and the world of the dead and eternity. Thoth became a moon god, creator of the earth, guardian of hieroglyphics as well as the god of scribes, Ra the sun god, Hathor goddess of the skies, Seth god of the desert, and Meretseger a god who loved silence because his heart did not beat.

A tribe of gods created by the imagination of Egyptians and a huge system of priests and ministers who attended to the divine multiplicity, arranged its sequence and rituals, and placed at its head the pharaoh, who possesed absolute power and therefore became a god in people's minds. The pharaonic kings were humans raised to divine rank, while gods took on material form and were shaped in the image of humans belonging to the everyday world. Hence the gods of the ancient Egyptians struggled among themselves, detested each other, fought, killed, and were born again "so that the tragedy could be repeated." Perhaps the legend of Iris and Osiris is one of the most powerful examples of gods struggling and making alliances, just as it splendidly represents anguished loss and vehement love and the resurrection that fertilizes life and kindles the adventure of eternal return. Isis says to Osiris:

Handsome young man, return to your house
I have not seen you for a long, long time
Oh master, distinguished among his ancestors
The first in his mother's stomach
Return to us in your original guise
(. . .) Return in safety, O first son of your father
Live in your house without fear
Your son Horus will protect you and avenge you
(. . .) I too long to see you
I, your sister Isis, who your heart loves
Your love stayed with me while you were far away
The land was drowned in tears that day.

This blend of the human and divine, the legendary and real, with veils of magic and breezes of poetry mixed in, confers on ancient Egyptian texts, both sacred and secular, a poetic aura, tightly interwoven with elements of the universe and phenomena of daily life that only acquire their 'true essence' in the realm of the divine and eternal. When pharaohs were poets they did not, despite their majesty and people deifying them, cease glorifying the gods who protected them. As I looked at Ramesses II in his modest, open sarcophagus, I recalled the glory attained with his victory over the Hittites in the Battle of Kadesh after a long war and fierce battle, of which the poets recounted his conquests, heroism, and his prayer to Amon requesting help in his ordeal, facing his enemies alone, in a manner that transformed the event into a legend that multiplied the victory's value and the heroic pharaoh's divinity. Ramesses said in his prayer to Amon, "What is it, oh father Amon? Is it possible for a father to forget his son? Have I ever done anything without you? In everything I have undertaken I have conducted myself according to your will. How great is your kindness! Who are these foreigners to you, oh Amon, these wretched men who don't know God? I have raised aloft many glorious deeds in your honor. I have filled your temple with prisoners. I have built an everlasting temple for you. I will offer a sacrifice of ten thousand bulls to you and send my ship far away to bring back treasures from remote lands. I seek refuge with you, O father Amon, as I stand amid my enemies who do not know you. Every nation has united against me and I am entirely alone. My soldiers have abandoned me and none of those in charge of the weapons on my boats came to my assistance."

The god Amon soon answered his call and Ramesses felt as though he was Mut, the goddess of war, and began killing his enemies until he was victorious.

In contrast to the historical account and what Ramesses II relates about himself, he looked to me, in his simple sarcophagus, stripped of royal halos and the embellishment of legends, like an ordinary person immersed in a humanity reminiscent of childhood innocence and unconcern. Perhaps I was moved because he stirred deep inside me the image of the child buried in the ground that prompted questions about existence, nonexistence, and continuing time and memory. But my wings were clipped and I didn't have any legends in which to swaddle the newborn baby to retrieve him from the cavern of extinction. Amon didn't know about me. Ra was "senile, his bones made of silver, his flesh of gold, his hair of lapis lazuli." Akhenaten's religion of love, peace, and pleasure had been dissipated and the priests recovered their strength and might after forcing his doctor to administer poison, which he drank while saying, "There is no place on earth for the kingdom of eternity. Everything will return to how it was. Fear, hatred, and darkness will reign over the world once more. It would be better if I had never been born so avoided knowing evil." The priests and their apparatus reverted to their original course: they sacrificed thousands of those who believed in Akhenaten's religion, flogged his servants, male and female alike, and forced them to work in stone quarries and build temples to rival gods.

Months had gone by since that visit but Ramesses II's face continued to visit me from time to time. When I couldn't sleep I would seek refuge in what I had written after the visit: "It is as though Ramesses is saying to us: Make a dream from your body and a body from your dream." The phrase was acrobatic in its intimations, but the difficult balance was appealing. One night I was woken a little before dawn by a violent gale and downpour of beans and chickpeas, as they say. I followed the sounds and things that suggested themselves to me through the long insomnia. I began to feel detached from my body. It began as a sensation and grew so I gave way to my feelings and wrote in a notebook:

"A cough. A murmur in the same place. I move as though I'm blind. Thoughts blaze. A flame inside grows bigger while a sensation sweeps over me: that my body is deserting me. But how can it when I'm wide awake, agitated, and following the noise and indications and ants crawling on the doorstep?

"I look at it again with pupils wide. There, stretched out with its familiar undulations. Or, rather, stealthily slipping away, leaving me as water without a container, blood without arteries, desire suspended in the dark unconscious.

"It's not possible, I tell myself. The body is always there; even when it no longer moves it can be looked at. But now I'm discovering it has gone. I feel bodiless, without an extension to confirm my outward existence, the existence of that bulk that gives me the illusion that I possess something of this world. I'm transformed into a mass of feelings and illusions. An eye looking out into a haze. A scattered spirit. A burning memory. Matter before creation. A voice without a tongue.

"That's all you are. You recall the fish that hatched lentils, the chicken that laid jam and chocolate, the sky that rained grilled locusts. You understand this when you are detached from your body. You pick up things that others can't see and say: Perhaps this 'system' is what the world is lacking. It seems that your body has deserted you, but maybe it's the body of other men and women. Your memory filled up and through its streams painted an illusory body, which you inhabited for a time, before the donors recalled their gifts. Look, your memory is full to the brim and you're lost in its hubbub, seeking help from a body of illusions. If it did not exist in the first place, how can it desert you?

"Think of yourself stripped of your body. The fleeting things in your imagination call to you from the balcony of paradise, waving tender fingertips, awakening saffron plants and camphor, and you feel a soft envelope wrapped around your ethereal being. You believe you have reached the lightness of happiness and intoxication of perfection and so abandoned your fleeing body and been left, perplexed and confused, listening to each of them whispering: 'Oh darling, what took you so long?'"

A Lady
Wrapped in Pride

I LIKE SEEING CAIRO from the Muqattam Hills: it appears clear and mysterious as my eyes wander over the dusty surface packed with remains and the minarets, domes, churches, graves, low-built houses, and tall buildings that come into view as the morning mist disperses.

On the Muqattam Hills I often get carried away recalling resplendent moments in Egypt's history. Her antiquities are unending: the Pyramids at Giza, Abu Simbel, verses from the Book of the Dead flowing on the surface of the Nile, the legend of Isis and Osiris, the Mosque of Amr ibn al-As, the exploits of the Fatimids, the towering Coptic churches, the mosques and inns of the Mamluks, the houses of Abd al-Rahman al-Harawi and al-Suhaymi and residence of Zaynab Khatun with their wooden oriels, decorative upper-door frames, upper women's quarters, men's reception rooms, and wooden engravings, al-Qarafa and its graves with chambers and courtyards to shelter the living dead. Can memory be repaired in the same way as antiquities, mosques, and churches to prevent those imprints that embody creativity, culture, and vision from disappearing?

On the Muqattam Hills I am oblivious to the clamor that immersed me before I reached this vast balcony, where I'm able to soar in an eternal time, plunging with it into what seems like a haze of beginning and end, enveloped in silence and reclusion. A self-contained existence that is indifferent to time and the moments dwelling deep within me. Always on these visits whispers circle inside me, like a conversation between me and the magical city. I say to myself, perhaps the Cairo period concealed in my adolescent memory since the 1950s is waking all of a sudden to remind me of what I lived in rapid sequence and then withdrew from, forgetting it and leaving it behind. Could I extend bridges once again to this space that my fickle emotions neglected? Why was I so eager to find Cairo as I wanted, ignoring the grooves drawn by time's fingers on my body and hers? Like a child who refuses to accept the death of things and beautiful memories, I always come to Cairo with fear and a choking feeling, as though I can hear a mocking voice: "What will you see this time?" "You're confident of your journey and permanence," I mutter defeated. "Will I continue in my prayers to you?" "Doubtful," the confident one replies. "Will words survive?" I ask. "Maybe," she answers smiling, "but I advise you to take refuge in forgetfulness once more in case you don't find what you want." I reply stubbornly, "I'll hang onto the words that come and go and reveal eternity in corners and lay bare what crouches in the unconscious. Through words and their nuances maybe I'll find a language that produces shades of meaning."

My voice forsakes me. The passion that I thought would grant me defiance and steadfastness abandons me and the choking returns, rising from the deepest place inside me, surrounding my vision, throttling my throat, and moistening my eyes with tears that circle in my sockets.

That remote evening in February at the end of the 1970s, gentle rain was stroking the ground, trees, and life, bringing refreshment to Cairo, which rarely saw winter. I was on my way down an alley situated off Doqqi's main street to visit Sitt Zaynat's house, where my two friends and I had lived in our last year of university. I'd only decided to make the visit that morning when I came across her daughter at EgyptAir. I had gone in to confirm my departure time and saw a flight attendant with wide, honey-colored eyes and a triangular-shaped face, which already showed signs of aging. I thought to myself that I knew this woman. I entered her office and explained what I wanted, then seized the opportunity, while she was absorbed in looking at dates, to ask her if she had studied at the Faculty of Arts at the end of the 1950s. After talking a little, I recalled Sayyida Afaf, who studied in the sociology department and graduated two years before me, and was Sitt Zaynat's daughter. She remembered me too and was very kind. I asked her about her mother and she told me that she still lived in the same house. She was ill, suffering from diabetes, and living with her sister. There was something broken in Afaf's voice, for I used to be amazed, as her neighbor, by her strong character, sharp beauty, and the way she jumped out of herself when she spoke. I did not wish to bombard her with questions so asked if it was possible to visit her mother. She welcomed the idea and said that it would make her mother happy.

The gentle rain that evening refreshed me and I thought to myself that this kind of gentle rain nourishes the earth and penetrates its depths. I was excited and slightly tense, for this visit put me before a period of my life that I still found enticing.

The alley was long and deep and still held on to its ancient trees despite some buildings having been erected where the old villas had stood. I was happy, as I walked along, that there were still trees in Doqqi, Mohandiseen, Giza, and Zamalek, even though these quarters had been overrun by cement. The buildings were new and some linden trees, willows, and acacias relieved the severity of the cars accumulated along the edges of the alleys and streets and the weight of the tall edifices squeezed together. It seemed to me that the alley preserved some of the rural feel that had characterized it in the 1960s. I proceeded slowly and could hear the sounds and din from the main street. But as I penetrated deeper into the alley I approached a tranquillity that was no longer possible in noisy, clamoring Cairo. A night oil lamp lighting the entrance to a two-story house came into view. Only the windows at the top were lit. The thin rain continued while the voice of a Qur'an reciter trailed off in the distance. A woman approaching sixty opened the door. "Excuse me, I would like to see Sitt Zaynat," I stammered. "Who shall I say has come, son?" she replied in a quiet voice.

"Mohamed from Morocco. I lived here twenty years ago."

Sitt Zaynat had not changed much. She had the same round face and wide eyes, her body preserved some of its fat, and the shawl round her head was the same. She was wearing a dark woollen pullover and had a white sheet over her legs. She sat on the sofa but showed clear signs of tiredness. After a short exchange she easily remembered which one I was of the three Moroccan students. I was the one responsible for paying the rent for the ground floor who would share a few friendly words with her, for at the time she always seemed very busy, telling the servant what needed to be done in the house, going out to buy food, preparing meals, and receiving visitors. After her husband died she had managed and supervised the affairs of her two daughters and son. The motherly tone and confidence I knew quickly returned, "Egypt rejoices. Praise God, Ustaz Mohamed is a bey and a university lecturer. How wonderful. What are your friends doing?"

I asked her about her health and she answered that it was not the best and praised God for everything. The daughter who worked at the airlines had lost her husband in the war of 1973 and now lived with her son in another apartment. The other daughter was a lawyer and was married and living in Alexandria, and her son, the youngest, worked for a company in the Gulf and would take the ground floor, which was locked up. Her sister lived with her as she was a widow and alone after her son was arrested for political activities. She sighed and added, "There's no security. Every day I say, God preserve us from disaster. Where have the good old days when you were students gone? My daughters have left home and they're always busy. My son has left the country and I only see him once a year. My health has declined and the country is not in a good way. Look at my poor sister. I feel my time is close. . . ."

When I listen to someone declaring they are waiting for death and that no one can do anything for them, I feel very uncomfortable. I have often avoided visiting people who are waiting for the end, even if I love them very much. I think that the situation is inhuman. How can you have a sincere conversation when one of you expects to die any minute and the other is enjoying life?

I tried to soothe Sitt Zaynat, pointing out that medicine has come a long way, life is in God's hands, and the great things she has achieved for her family. She should relax and not worry about what is going on around her. She responded in a sad tone, "Of course, I have great faith in God but I still feel sad. I married when I was eighteen. My parents and my husband didn't let me finish my education. That's why I wanted my children to finish university. I didn't want to marry again after my husband died. But after all this effort and hope, I look and find that all good things disappear and people run around not knowing where they are going. I only see my children on special occasions. But I praise

168

God and thank Him. Believe me, I'm not afraid of death. It seems to me that's where I'll recover peace of mind and security."

I changed the subject. "God forbid. Your children need you and I will come to visit you every year. People should be optimistic. I wanted to ask you about Umm Fathiya. Has she visited?" Sitt Zaynat said, "She hasn't been round for ages. That woman is a princess. She always reminisces about the days she worked for you. Who knows, maybe she'll beat me to the next world. I'll give her your regards there. . . ."

I was ready to stay with Sitt Zaynat for as long as possible. Our conversation created an unexpected intimacy and I found it strange that I had not discovered her vibrant personality, which words can't describe, when I was a student. Maybe it was because I saw myself as passing through, bound to Cairo's sparkle and the lure of cultural life. When I listened to her reminding me about bread and salt and recalling the day we slaughtered the animal for Eid and her prayers for our success, I felt small, for I'd lived next door to this kind woman for a year while studying without ever really getting to know her. I didn't accept her invitation for dinner. I was overwhelmed by a burning inside me and my emotions were on fire. I said goodbye and promised to visit again. In the long alley, as I walked through the gentle rain, I felt as though my other self, the person I was at the end of the 1950s, had become separated from me. It was as though it had stepped out of my body and was walking beside me, cheerful and intoxicated in this space, which had survived despite everything. It walked next to me, not paying any attention to my slow, stumbling steps, looking up at the windows and turning in every direction, aroused by feelings and obscure thoughts. My other self was energetic and confident that it would grasp the unknown that was tempting it with discovery and adventure at the time. Things that I'd forgotten came to me in succession to furnish a dull present that was surrounded in ashes. I said to myself that the past could save us despite our obsession with a blurred future.

In the hotel I asked room service to bring my food to the room and began reading a French book entitled *Conditional Freedom* in which the author relates her experience with a prisoner was been sentenced to twenty years for murder. She became acquainted with him through correspondence after receiving a letter from prison commenting on a study she had published in a journal about the novelist George Sand. She found the author of the comments was unusually sensitive and very perceptive and had enriched her—the specialist in George Sand's literature. They began writing to each other and then met up. I used to, and still do, keep texts to read when I feel a wave of depression or that things have lost meaning. Through them I can escape the pressure and enter the world of slumber.

◎

I saw myself peering across intertwining alleys during the afternoon rest, at least I presumed this was the time as a group of people looked like they were relaxing in the bright sunlight that was shining on parts of the alleys. I was turning around with my head raised to the sky, as though gazing up at the minaret of the Mosque of Sulayman. Oh! What brought me here? I remembered reading about a woman who rented a furnished room in an ancient house, which had been renovated in the style of Fatimid architecture. I decided to go there myself. Perhaps the migration would remove me from the clamor suffocating me. I carried on walking, finding the emptiness of the alleys strange as the midday lull did not usually mean nobody at all would be in the street. I saw a sign on a large door: "Furnished rooms for rent. Antique furniture. Glass windows. Perfect quiet." I lifted the latch to knock on the door and it was opened by a doorman wearing a white gallabiya and yellow striped turban. He smiled without saying anything and gestured to me to enter. The hall was long and led into a parlor, which was overlooked by a balcony with dark wooden railings. On the two sides of the parlor there were pools surrounded by small trees and flowers, and there was a fountain attached to the left wall. A freshness emanated from this retreat, opening onto a clear sky. I proceeded slowly, looking up at the balcony. After a little while a dignified lady appeared, wearing what looked like a kaftan with a turquoise scarf on her head. Her eyes were wide and almond-shaped and emitted a special magic. I continued with my head raised up at her while she looked down with her hands on the edge of the railings. "I'm looking for a room," I stammered.

She gestured to the steps with her hand and I ascended to the balcony, which led into a large hall, and followed the woman to her seat. She looked at me for a while then said, "Are you sure it's a room you're looking for?"

"Of course. I'd like a quiet room."

She replied with a slight smile, "Your eyes seem to be looking for something else."

I noticed—though it was difficult to tell how old she was— that she possessed a captivating beauty that instilled a certain awe. What do you say to a beautiful, awesome, seemingly rich woman when you don't know what will please her? Her confidence confused me and stirred my curiosity and I forgot about the room. I waited for her to speak. After a short silence she said, "There are quiet rooms everywhere. But this large house, I don't rent its rooms simply to live in. I don't take money from residents. I want something else."

"Like what?"

"Everyone presents something he possesses."

I was not expecting this kind of conversation. Was I in a maze and this its guard testing me with ambiguous questions?

I thought for a moment.

"So you aren't of the view that we don't really own anything except what we've lost?"

"Maybe. What have you lost that you think you possess now?"

"It is difficult to define final loss."

"Why, then, do you cite a view that is no use to you?"

"Actually I feel that what I have lost is still close to me, as though part of my inner world."

"Like what?"

"My mother is dead but I feel her present in me."

"Maybe it is she who owns you?"

I didn't feel the woman was mocking or criticizing me so I said, "Perhaps. I feel the same about Umm Fathiya, who I can't find."

"Who is Umm Fathiya?"

"You would love her if you knew her. Maybe you could make her a housekeeper in this charming house."

"Is this all you have?"

"There are other men and women whom I've lost. People who have a special place inside me, whom I long for but who have gone away or died. Women who disperse the emptiness of the world and fill it with splendor and life. I usually only knew them for a moment: in a café in the rain, an evening never to be repeated, in a city garden I never visited again. I feel the presence of such moments constantly and indulge in others similar to them. They are lost moments but I possess them through their hidden presence in me. I'm often blown away by their intoxicating scent."

"Praise God, I didn't imagine that you were such a romantic."

"It is not what you think. With a beautiful and intelligent woman I can only speak in this language. You determine its rhythm."

"Do you think you can invade my heart with such talk? I'm past the age of fleeting attachments and adventures. I'm aware I possess the remnants of irresistible beauty but I don't respond to admirers' attempts to seduce me. I might enjoy them flirting as it makes me love myself more, but I don't expect anything further."

"You're entitled to be arrogant and your lovers are entitled to crowd around. Why haven't I seen you before? I often walk around this area."

"I don't leave this big house. I'm used to waiting and forgiving those who turn a blind eye when they pass my door. I stay up all night. My house is open to all kinds of people: good and evil, peace lovers and murderers, poets and boors, old and young, people looking for company and people looking for oblivion . . . all the same."

"Really, you want to possess everything."

"That's not what I'm after. I own a big house and insomnia drives the sleep from my eyes. Loneliness is scary but I can't exist anywhere but in this place that envelops me and that I envelop. I wait for people seeking rooms so that I can travel to other places through talking to them."

"So having people around stops you being lonely?"

"Amid the crowds of residents and their language and flirting I can recall my life's tune. Through them I'm able to survive, though they don't realize it. They think it's me who gives them a reason to go on."

"I too feel like you're a guardian angel guiding my steps in this midday heat."

"Are you being romantic again? I won't be able to give you the room you're looking for."

"No. I beg you. . . ."

I woke up shouting and begging the awesome woman not to deprive me of the shelter of one of her rooms.

This strange dream stuck in my mind. It seemed to embody Jung's archetype, which lives in the depths of the unconscious and makes us pursue it or draw inspiration from it without us understanding it or comprehending its symbols and constituent elements.

This dream, which appeared scattered before me and extended into some of my daydreams, escaped me whenever I thought I'd grasped it. Its basic elements almost never changed: an impregnable woman draped in arrogance, a space emitting an attractive ancientness that tempted you into confession, talk that lived outside language.

I'm still baffled by the incomplete dream and wait for it to come back so I can ask the beautiful woman what possessions other people have brought to her. Was she a guardian angel to everyone to whom she gave shelter?

Thinking of this dream-woman now, I remember what Kafka said in another context: "Sometimes, in her pride, she fears for the world more than for herself."

Author's Notes

For some of the history of ancient Egypt I used the following books:

Dictionary of Ancient Egyptian Civilisation (various authors), trans. Amin Salama (General Book Organization)

Otto Neubert, *La vallée des Rois*, ed. R. Lafont (1954).

Christiane Desroches Noblecourt, *Ramsés II (La veritable histoire)*, Livre de Poche, no. 14331.

Sacred and Religious Texts of Ancient Egypt, 2 vols., Arabic translation (UNESCO, 1984).

Some phrases at the end of the chapter "A Pharaoh in a Cotton Shroud" have been borrowed from *The Book of Imagination* by al-Muhasibi.

Glossary

Abdullah Nadim (d. 1896) a writer, journalist, orator, and nationalist who was forced to spend many years in hiding after the failure of the 'Urabi revolt (1879–82).

Baath Party a political movement, especially influential in Syria and Iraq, founded on principles of socialism, nationalism, and pan-Arabism.

Eid al-Adha Festival of Sacrifice. A religious festival celebrated by Muslims commemorating Abraham's willingness to sacrifice his son.

Farag Fuda Egyptian academic, assassinated by Islamic fundamentalists in 1992.

futuwwa strongmen. In the Middle Ages the futuwwa were groups of chivalrous young men who maintained order in the city quarters. By the nineteenth century these groups had become gangs of thugs.

fuul fava beans, an Egyptian staple flavored with oil, lemon juice, and seasoning.

gallabiya loose, shirt-like garment worn by peasants in Egypt.

harafish society's underclass; also, vagabonds or ruffians. Naguib Mahfouz and his friends used to refer to their group as "the harafish."

ifreet an evil spirit in Arabian mythology.

infitah President Sadat's policy of 'opening up' Egypt to private and foreign investment.

jinn a supernatural creature, which can be either good or evil.

Kalila wa Dimna a well-known collection of fables about people and animals.

karkadeh a drink made with hibiscus.

koshari a staple dish of macaroni, rice, lentils, chickpeas, and tomato sauce.

milaya a wrap worn by Egyptian women.

Nasr Hamid Abu Zayd (b. 1943) an Egyptian liberal religious thinker who suffered persecution because of his approach to the Qur'an and views on religious discourse.

Nasser's speech at the Azhar Mosque famous speech made by Egyptian President Nasser on Friday November 9, 1956 decrying the invasion of the Suez Canal by Britain, France and Israel.

qanun a stringed instrument resembling a zither.

Said Mahran the protagonist in Naguib Mahfouz's novel *The Thief and the Dogs*.

salep a drink made from grinding the tubers of orchids.

Sheikh al-Junaydi the Sufi mentor of Said Mahran in Naguib Mahfouz's novel *The Thief and the Dogs*.

umma the Muslim community.

ustaz a form of address to intellectuals.

Translator's Note

MOHAMED BERRADA WAS BORN in Rabat on May 14, 1938. He spent his childhood in Fez, where he attended one of the 'free' schools set up by the Moroccan Nationalist Movement to resist the French mandate. In 1955, at the age of seventeen, he packed his bags and headed for Egypt to continue his studies in Arabic, for in Morocco at the time higher education was conducted in the language of the occupier. In Egypt he completed an initial matriculation year before embarking on a degree in Arabic literature at Cairo University. Then, in 1960, he returned to Morocco and found work with the Moroccan National Broadcasting Corporation. He immediately became involved in the cultural scene, helping to found the Moroccan Writers' Union in 1961, which he would serve as president between 1976 and 1983. In 1964 he re-immersed himself in academia, taking up a teaching post at Muhammad V University in Rabat. In 1970 he traveled to France and spent three years at the Sorbonne writing a thesis on

Muhammad Mandour and Arabic literary criticism. On returning to Morocco, he was appointed Professor of Modern Arabic Literature at Muhammad V University, a post he held until he retired in the late 1990s. Throughout this period he continued to be heavily involved in Arab culture and literary affairs, writing regularly in the press, publishing novels and short stories, and attending conferences and seminars across the Arab world. He now lives in Paris with his wife, Leila Shahid.

This short biography of the author's life suggests an immediate affinity with the protagonist of *Like a Summer Never to Be Repeated*. The book is loosely based around the author's own memories of Egypt over a period of four decades, from 1955 to the late 1990s, the time of writing. Thus the reader follows its protagonist, Hammad (or Mohamed as he becomes in the second part of the book), through his student days in Cairo—hanging out with friends, getting up to mischief, discovering the city's secret haunts, revising for exams, and falling under the spell of Gamal Abd al-Nasser—to his experiences as a visiting intellectual, when he came to Cairo to attend conferences, meet up with friends, and renew his links with the city he fell in love with as a child, watching films like *Bab al-Hadid* and *Love and Revenge*.

The fictional façade naturally raises questions. Why present one's story as belonging to another, imaginary character? This is not the only question the reader of *Like a Summer* is likely to ask himself, for every page of the book is an invitation to think and reflect. Sometimes the process is initiated by the narrator, as he tries to fathom the logic (or illogic) of memory, ponders the relationship between the past and the present, debates issues of literary criticism, or strays into philosophizing. Other times the questions are born in the mind of the reader as the narrative switches between different spaces, times, and modes. Why does the text start out in the third person then change halfway to the first person? Is the book a novel, a memoir, a new kind of literary criticism? How are we meant to understand the juxtaposition of the real and the unreal? Why is the narrative presented piece-meal, full of gaps and unresolved issues?

The key to some of the answers, I believe, lies in the author's conception of literature and the postmodern sentiment that lies behind the text. Writing, for Berrada, is "a complex, playful process that incorporates the imagined as well as the real." The novel, as he conceives it, is a constantly evolving form. Thus the blend of anecdote, autobiography, literary criticism, philosophy, dream narrative, and elements of surrealism in *Like A Summer* is intended to test the boundaries of novel writing. Moreover, since history, including personal history, is always a construct, foregrounding the narrative element of autobiography is surely a more honest way of approaching a personal story. Rather than presenting his memories as truth, which is subject to suspicion, Berrada presents them as fiction and leaves it to the reader to decide where reality and imagination begin and end. In the spirit of postmodernist writing the author is playing with us, challenging us to rethink our assumptions about literature and literary categories. But there is also a serious message here, for the dis-jointed nature of the text—the mixture of styles—and split in the protagonist between the third-person Hammad and first-person narrator (Mohamed) embody the loss of cohesion, the fragmen-tation of the grand Arab dream, and the dislocation between the past and the present in the mind of the author. The focal point of the story, as the title suggests, is the magical summer of 1956, when Hammad passed the exam that would enable him to enter Cairo University, Morocco gained independence, and Nasser announced the nationalization of the Suez Canal. The future looked bright: the Arabs were entering a new era, one that prom-ised social justice, freedom, and solidarity in the face of foreign hegemony, and Hammad and his friends were embarking on the most exciting period of their lives. But events unfolded onto

180

depression and defeat, thus the trip down memory lane in *Like a Summer* is really an attempt on the part of Berrada to reconcile an optimistic past with a disappointing present.

The disappointment and nostalgia that pervade the narrative do not, however, make *Like a Summer* any less charming a read. From schoolboy pranks to comic romantic situations and awkward moments at conferences, the book is full of laughter and humor, while the author's deep love and knowledge of Cairo shines through his descriptions of intimate scenes of the city and lovable characters like Umm Fathiya. *Like a Summer* is an affectionate tribute to Egypt and Egyptian culture—a testimony to the formative role it played in the life of the author and an acknowledgment of its pioneering role in modern Arabic culture and destiny.

Like a Summer Never to Be Repeated is Berrada's third novel. By the time it was published in 1999, the author was already famous across the Arab world for his fiction and nonfiction. He is credited with introducing French literary theory to Arabic-speaking audiences through his translations and critical writings, and his first two novels, *The Game of Forgetting* and *Fugitive Light*, received critical acclaim and were hailed as important contributions to the experimental Arabic novel. In 1999 he was awarded the Moroccan Order of Merit for Literature.

In terms of translation, *Like a Summer*, with its variety of styles and often abstract language, posed something of a challenge. Nevertheless, it has been my great pleasure to work on this unusual and highly experimental text. Literary translation is always, in the end, interpretation, and I can only hope that my interpretation does justice to the original.

Finally, I would like to express my deep gratitude to Sabry Hafez, Feras Hamza, Muaadh Salih, Nicola Antaki, and the author himself for their invaluable help over the past year.

181

Modern Arabic Literature

The American University in Cairo Press is the world's leading publisher of Arabic literature in translation.

For a full list of available titles, please go to:

mal.aucpress.com